D0953670

My Little Pony

Adventures in Friendship

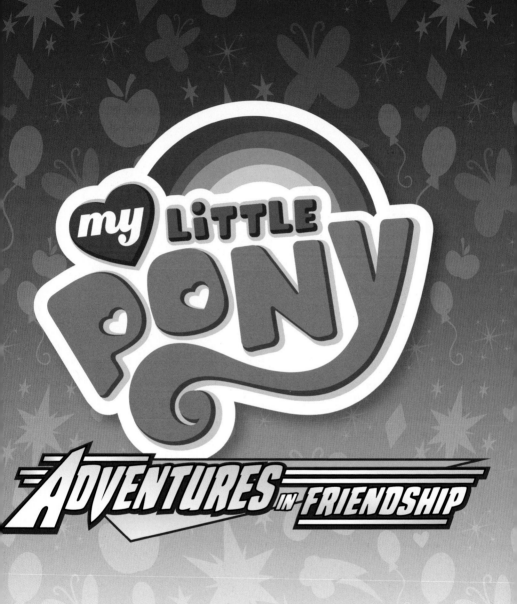

COVER BY **SARA RICHARD**

ORIGINAL SERIES EDITS BY **BOBBY CURNOW**

COLLECTION EDITS BY **JUSTIN EISINGER** AND **ALONZO SIMON**

COLLECTION DESIGN BY **THOM ZAHLER**

Special thanks to Brian Lenard, Ed Lane and Michael Kelly for their invaluable assistance.

ISBN: 978-1-63140-466-5   18 17 16 15   1 2 3 4

Ted Adams, CEO & Publisher
Greg Goldstein, President & COO
Robbie Robbins, EVP/Sr. Graphic Artist
Chris Ryall, Chief Creative Officer/Editor-in-Chief
Matthew Ruzicka, CPA, Chief Financial Officer
Alan Payne, VP of Sales
Dirk Wood, VP of Marketing
Lorelei Bunjes, VP of Digital Services
Jeff Webber, VP of Digital Publishing & Business Development

IDW ® Licensed By:

www.IDWPUBLISHING.com
IDW founded by Ted Adams, Alex Garner, Kris Oprisko, and Robbie Robbins

Facebook: **facebook.com/idwpublishing**
Twitter: **@idwpublishing**
YouTube: **youtube.com/idwpublishing**
Tumblr: **tumblr.idwpublishing.com**
Instagram: **instagram.com/idwpublishing**

MY LITTLE PONY: ADVENTURES IN FRIENDSHIP, VOLUME 4. NOVEMBER 2015. FIRST PRINTING. HASBRO and its logo, MY LITTLE PONY, and all related characters are trademarks of Hasbro and are used with permission. © 2015 Hasbro. All Rights Reserved. The IDW logo is registered in the U.S. Patent and Trademark Office. IDW Publishing, a division of Idea and Design Works, LLC. Editorial offices: 2765 Truxtun Road, San Diego, CA 92106. Any similarities to persons living or dead are purely coincidental. With the exception of artwork used for review purposes, none of the contents of this publication may be reprinted without the permission of Idea and Design Works, LLC. Printed in Korea.
IDW Publishing does not read or accept unsolicited submissions of ideas, stories, or artwork.

Originally published as MY LITTLE PONY: FRIENDS FOREVER issues #2, 7, and 20.

CHAPTER ONE

DISCORD

WRITTEN BY **JEREMY WHITLEY**
ART BY **TONY FLEECS**
COLOR FLATS BY **LAUREN PERRY**
LETTERS BY **NEIL UYETAKE**

CHAPTER TWO

PRINCESS LUNA

WRITTEN BY **JEREMY WHITLEY**
ART BY **TONY FLEECS**
COLORS BY **HEATHER BRECKEL**
LETTERS BY **NEIL UYETAKE**

CHAPTER THREE

DISCORD AND PRINCESS LUNA

WRITTEN BY **JEREMY WHITLEY**
ART BY **BRENDA HICKEY**
COLORS BY **HEATHER BRECKEL**
LETTERS BY **NEIL UYETAKE**

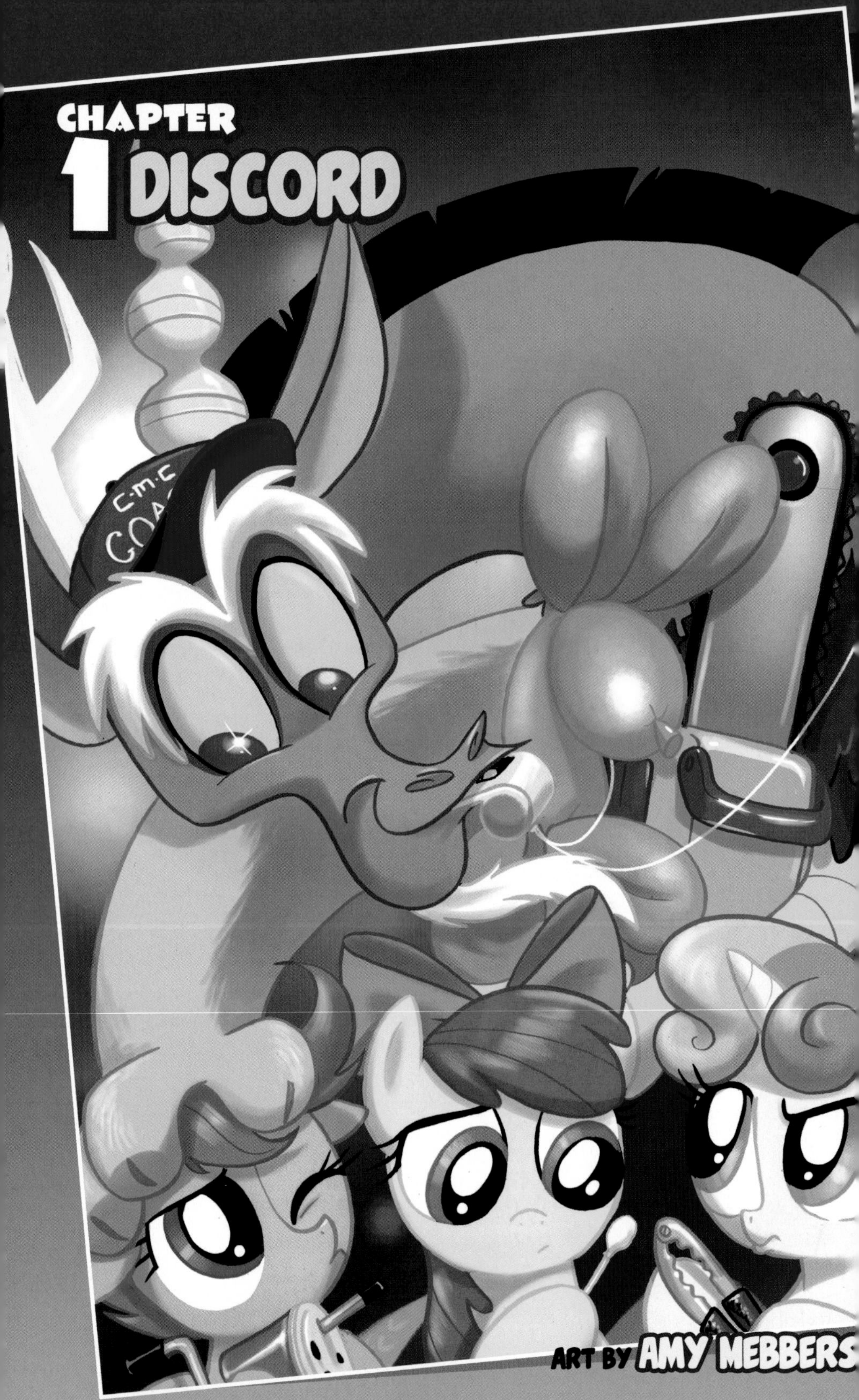
CHAPTER
1 DISCORD
C·M·C
GOA
ART BY AMY MEBBERS

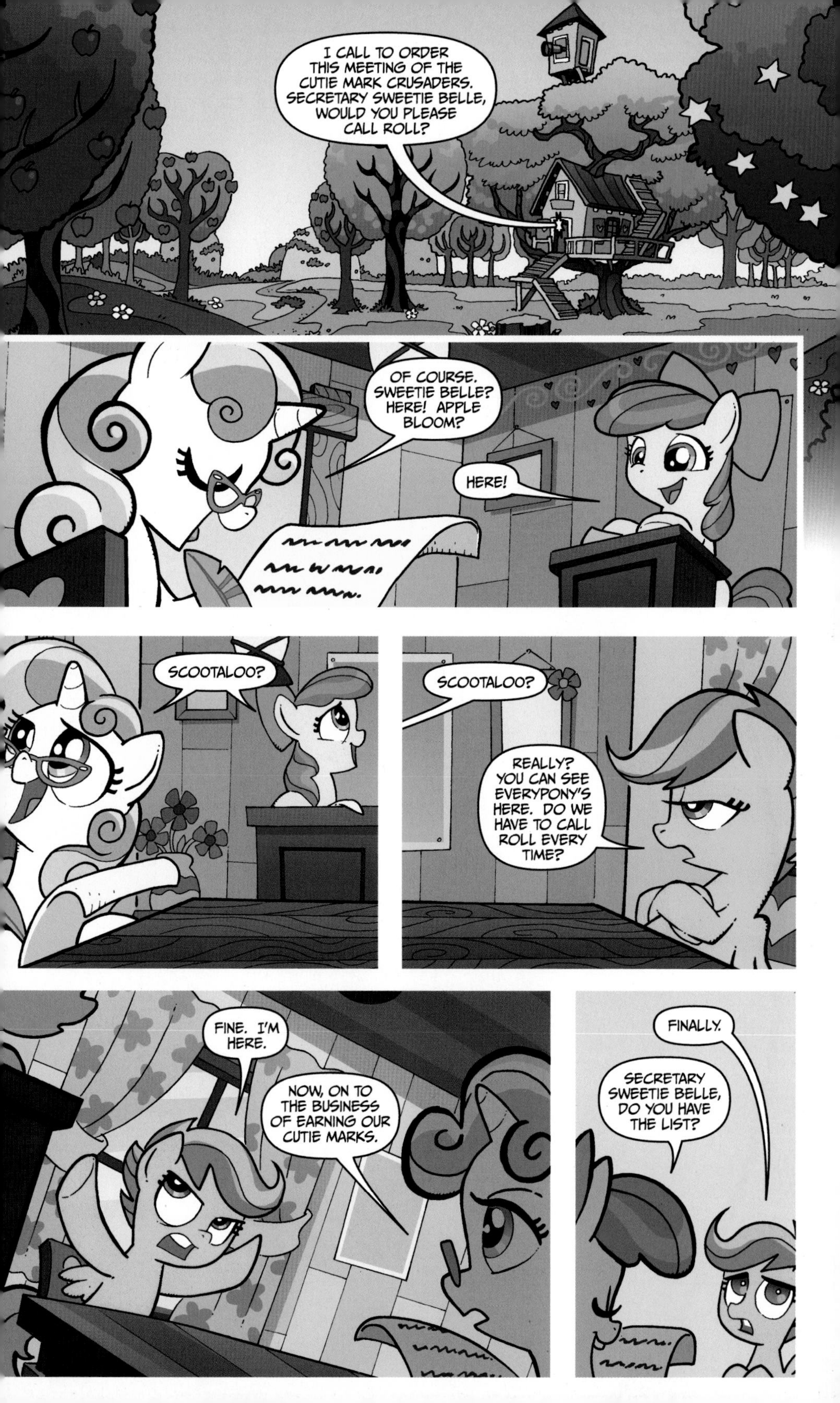
I CALL TO ORDER THIS MEETING OF THE CUTIE MARK CRUSADERS. SECRETARY SWEETIE BELLE, WOULD YOU PLEASE CALL ROLL?
OF COURSE. SWEETIE BELLE? HERE! APPLE BLOOM?
HERE!
SCOOTALOO?
SCOOTALOO?
REALLY? YOU CAN SEE EVERYPONY'S HERE. DO WE HAVE TO CALL ROLL EVERY TIME?
FINE. I'M HERE.
NOW, ON TO THE BUSINESS OF EARNING OUR CUTIE MARKS.
FINALLY.
SECRETARY SWEETIE BELLE, DO YOU HAVE THE LIST?

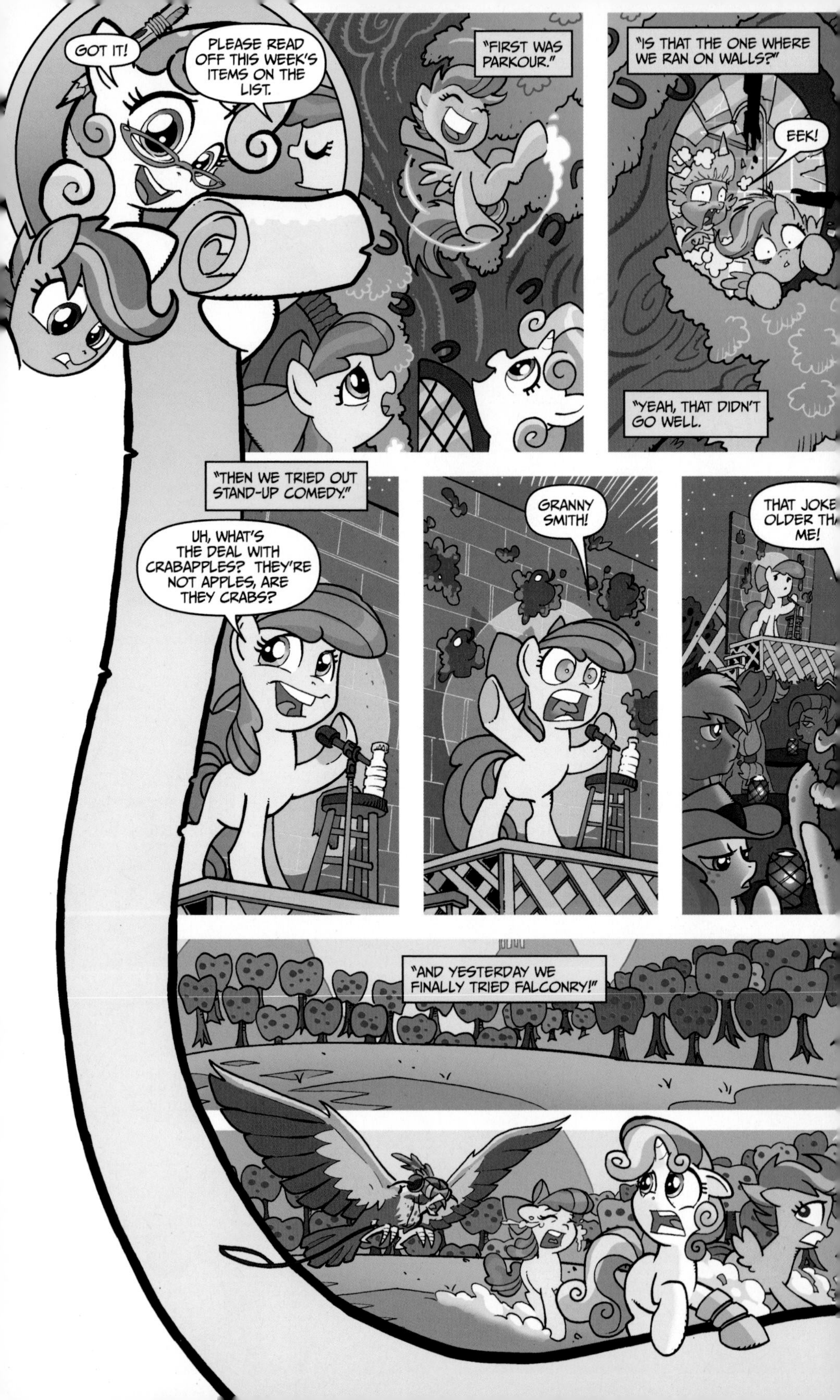
GOT IT!
PLEASE READ OFF THIS WEEK'S ITEMS ON THE LIST.
"FIRST WAS PARKOUR."
"IS THAT THE ONE WHERE WE RAN ON WALLS?"
EEK!
"YEAH, THAT DIDN'T GO WELL.
"THEN WE TRIED OUT STAND-UP COMEDY."
UH, WHAT'S THE DEAL WITH CRABAPPLES? THEY'RE NOT APPLES, ARE THEY CRABS?
GRANNY SMITH!
"AND YESTERDAY WE FINALLY TRIED FALCONRY!"

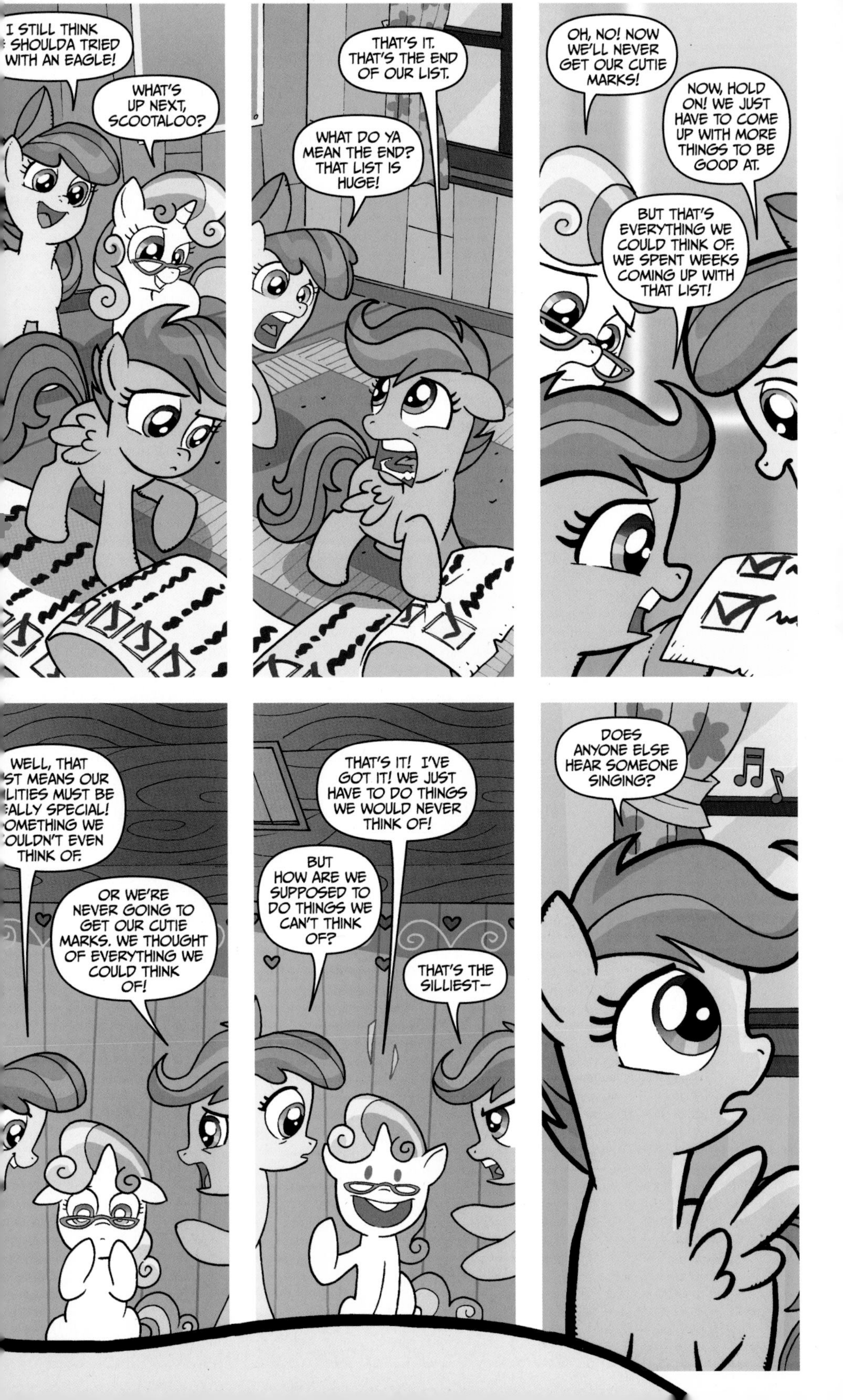
I STILL THINK
SHOULDA TRIED
WITH AN EAGLE!
WHAT'S
UP NEXT,
SCOOTALOO?
THAT'S IT.
THAT'S THE END
OF OUR LIST.
WHAT DO YA
MEAN THE END?
THAT LIST IS
HUGE!
OH, NO! NOW
WE'LL NEVER
GET OUR CUTIE
MARKS!
NOW, HOLD
ON! WE JUST
HAVE TO COME
UP WITH MORE
THINGS TO BE
GOOD AT.
BUT THAT'S
EVERYTHING WE
COULD THINK OF.
WE SPENT WEEKS
COMING UP WITH
THAT LIST!
WELL, THAT
ST MEANS OUR
LITIES MUST BE
ALLY SPECIAL!
OMETHING WE
OULDN'T EVEN
THINK OF.
OR WE'RE
NEVER GOING TO
GET OUR CUTIE
MARKS. WE THOUGHT
OF EVERYTHING WE
COULD THINK
OF!
THAT'S IT! I'VE
GOT IT! WE JUST
HAVE TO DO THINGS
WE WOULD NEVER
THINK OF!
BUT
HOW ARE WE
SUPPOSED TO
DO THINGS WE
CAN'T THINK
OF?
THAT'S THE
SILLIEST—
DOES
ANYONE ELSE
HEAR SOMEONE
SINGING?

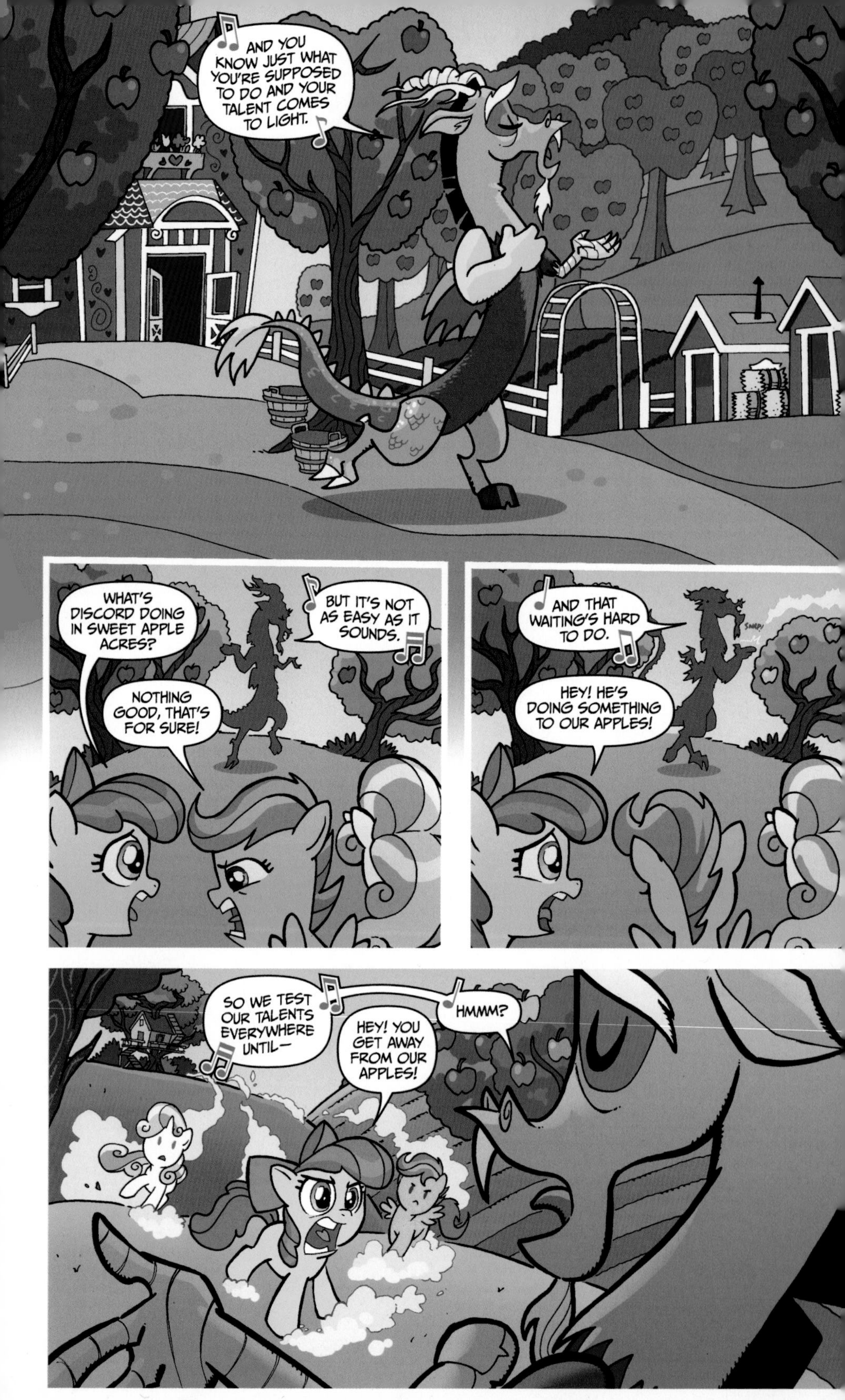
AND YOU KNOW JUST WHAT YOU'RE SUPPOSED TO DO AND YOUR TALENT COMES TO LIGHT.
WHAT'S DISCORD DOING IN SWEET APPLE ACRES?
BUT IT'S NOT AS EASY AS IT SOUNDS.
NOTHING GOOD, THAT'S FOR SURE!
AND THAT WAITING'S HARD TO DO.
SNAP!
HEY! HE'S DOING SOMETHING TO OUR APPLES!
SO WE TEST OUR TALENTS EVERYWHERE UNTIL—
HEY! YOU GET AWAY FROM OUR APPLES!
HMMM?

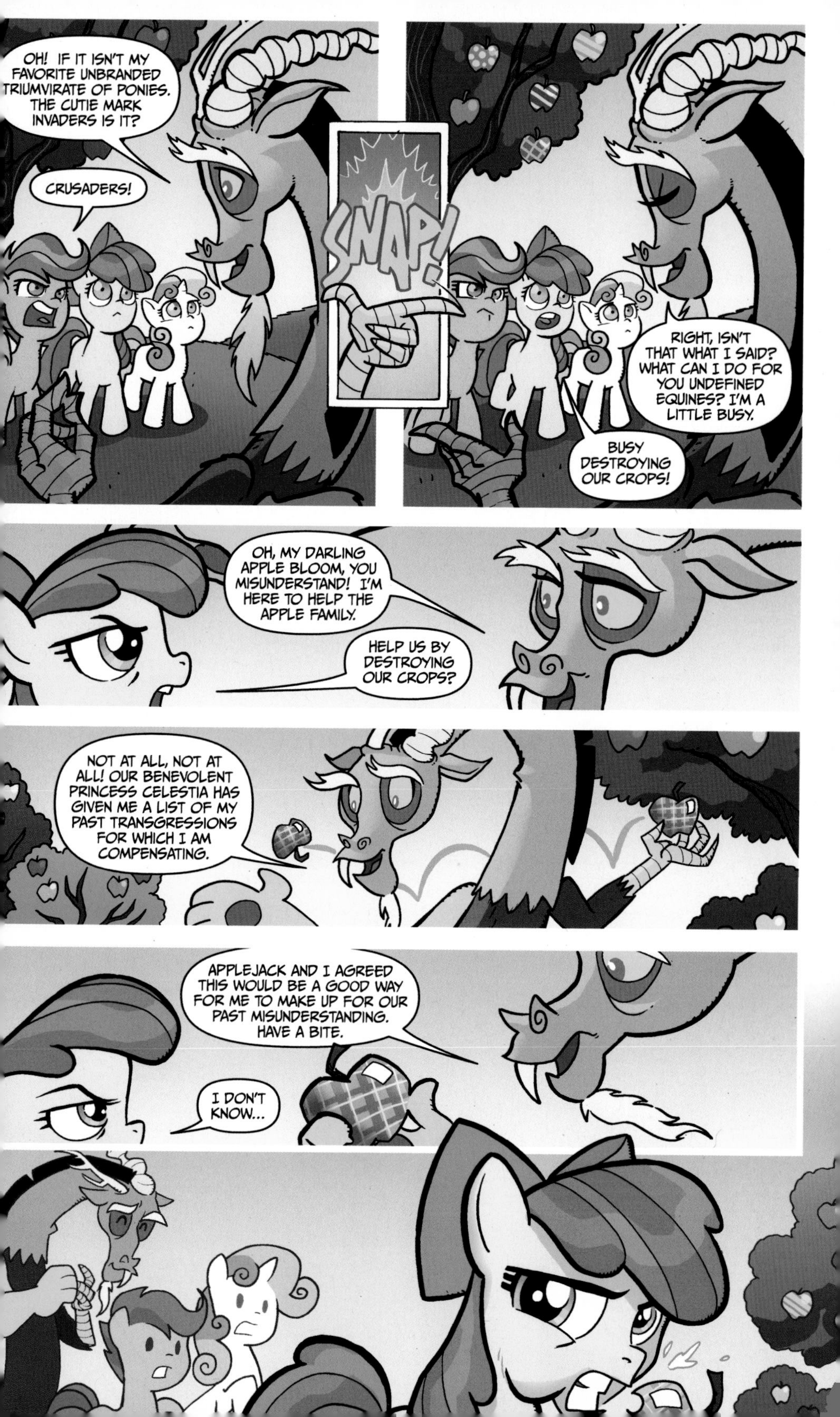
OH! IF IT ISN'T MY FAVORITE UNBRANDED TRIUMVIRATE OF PONIES. THE CUTIE MARK INVADERS IS IT?
CRUSADERS!
SNAP!
RIGHT, ISN'T THAT WHAT I SAID? WHAT CAN I DO FOR YOU UNDEFINED EQUINES? I'M A LITTLE BUSY.
BUSY DESTROYING OUR CROPS!
OH, MY DARLING APPLE BLOOM, YOU MISUNDERSTAND! I'M HERE TO HELP THE APPLE FAMILY.
HELP US BY DESTROYING OUR CROPS?
NOT AT ALL, NOT AT ALL! OUR BENEVOLENT PRINCESS CELESTIA HAS GIVEN ME A LIST OF MY PAST TRANSGRESSIONS FOR WHICH I AM COMPENSATING.
APPLEJACK AND I AGREED THIS WOULD BE A GOOD WAY FOR ME TO MAKE UP FOR OUR PAST MISUNDERSTANDING. HAVE A BITE.
I DON'T KNOW...

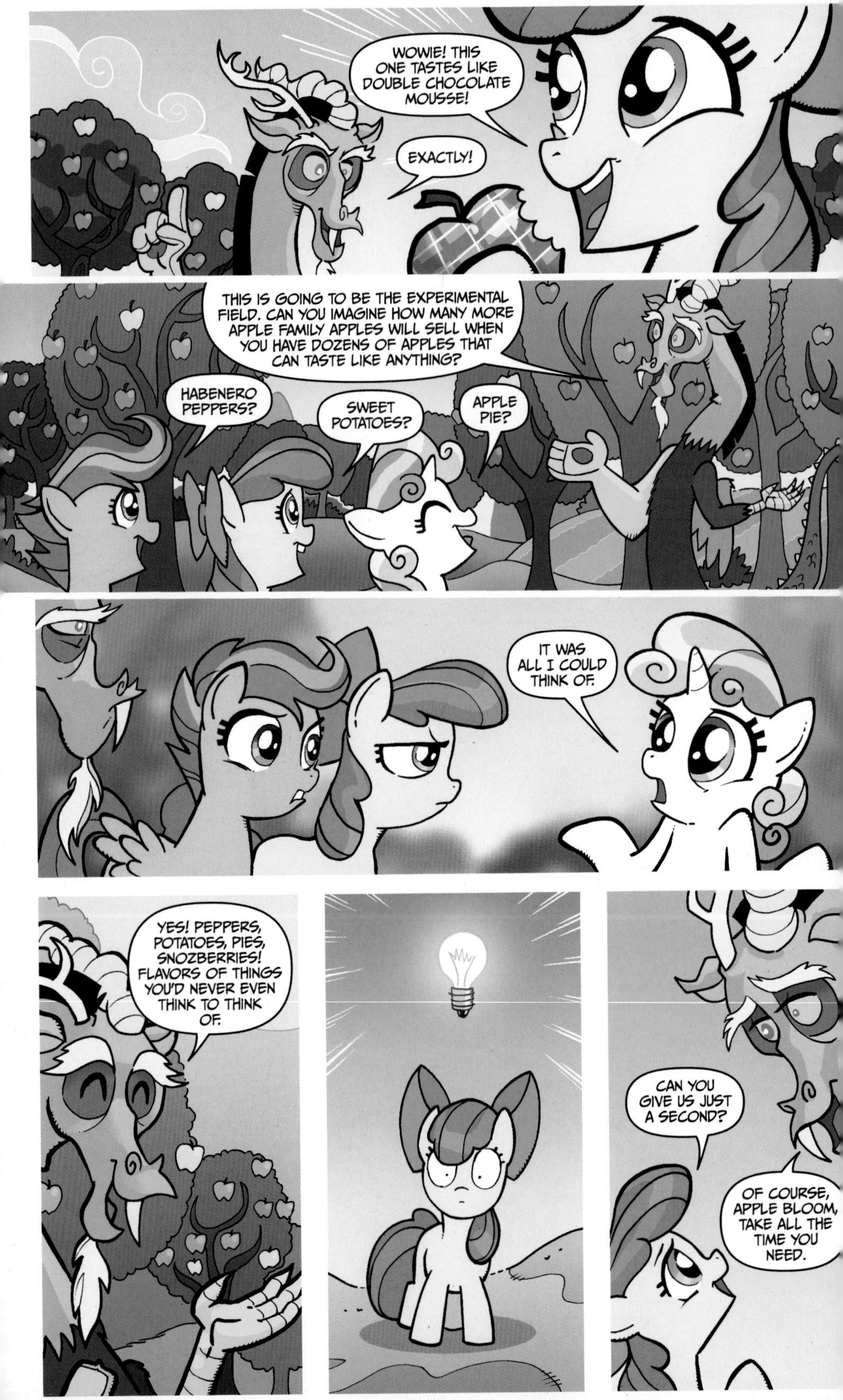
WOWIE! THIS ONE TASTES LIKE DOUBLE CHOCOLATE MOUSSE!
EXACTLY!
THIS IS GOING TO BE THE EXPERIMENTAL FIELD. CAN YOU IMAGINE HOW MANY MORE APPLE FAMILY APPLES WILL SELL WHEN YOU HAVE DOZENS OF APPLES THAT CAN TASTE LIKE ANYTHING?
HABENERO PEPPERS?
SWEET POTATOES?
APPLE PIE?
IT WAS ALL I COULD THINK OF.
YES! PEPPERS, POTATOES, PIES, SNOZBERRIES! FLAVORS OF THINGS YOU'D NEVER EVEN THINK TO THINK OF.
CAN YOU GIVE US JUST A SECOND?
OF COURSE, APPLE BLOOM, TAKE ALL THE TIME YOU NEED.

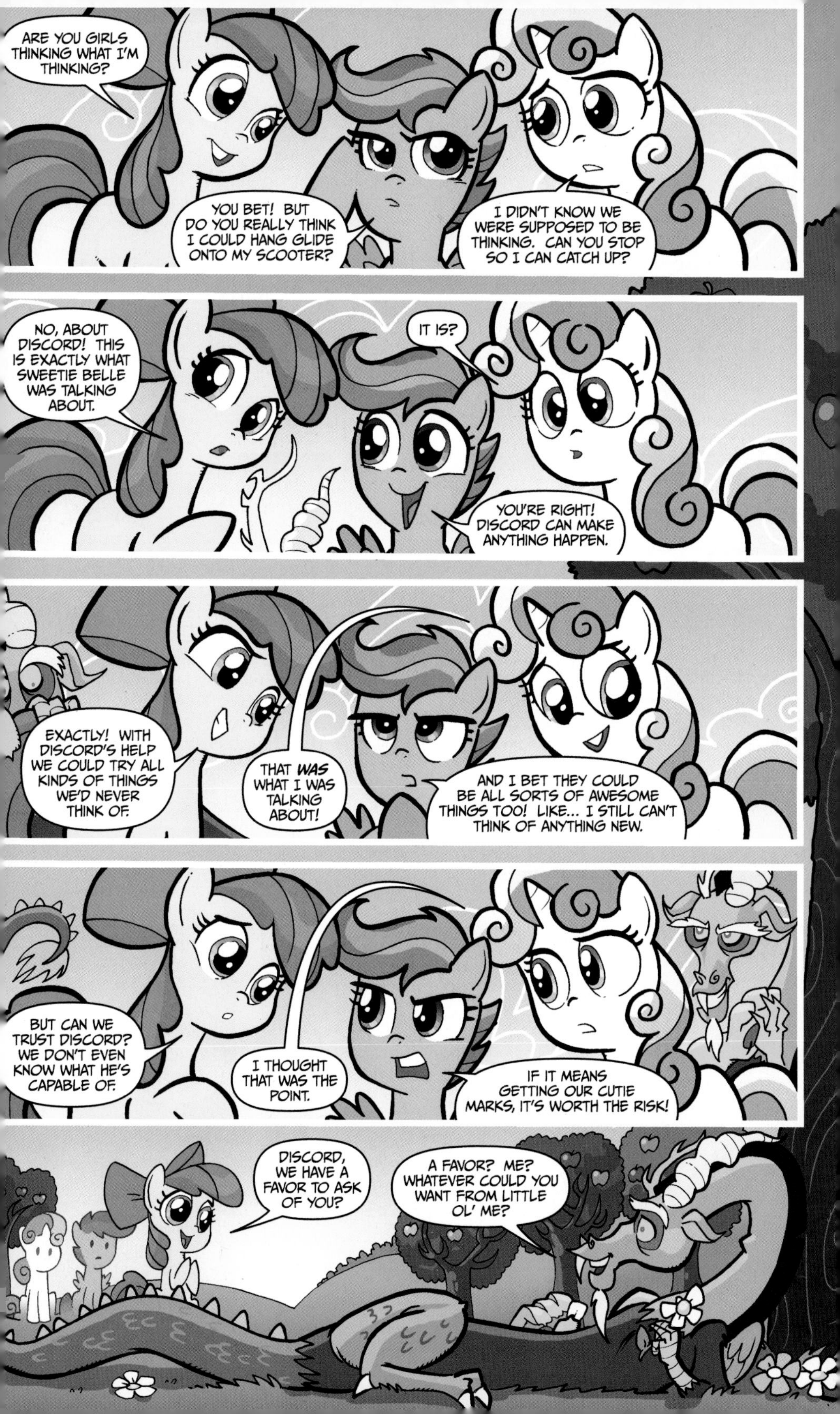

ARE YOU GIRLS THINKING WHAT I'M THINKING?
YOU BET! BUT DO YOU REALLY THINK I COULD HANG GLIDE ONTO MY SCOOTER?
I DIDN'T KNOW WE WERE SUPPOSED TO BE THINKING. CAN YOU STOP SO I CAN CATCH UP?
NO, ABOUT DISCORD! THIS IS EXACTLY WHAT SWEETIE BELLE WAS TALKING ABOUT.
IT IS?
YOU'RE RIGHT! DISCORD CAN MAKE ANYTHING HAPPEN.
EXACTLY! WITH DISCORD'S HELP WE COULD TRY ALL KINDS OF THINGS WE'D NEVER THINK OF.
THAT *WAS* WHAT I WAS TALKING ABOUT!
AND I BET THEY COULD BE ALL SORTS OF AWESOME THINGS TOO! LIKE... I STILL CAN'T THINK OF ANYTHING NEW.
BUT CAN WE TRUST DISCORD? WE DON'T EVEN KNOW WHAT HE'S CAPABLE OF.
I THOUGHT THAT WAS THE POINT.
IF IT MEANS GETTING OUR CUTIE MARKS, IT'S WORTH THE RISK!
DISCORD, WE HAVE A FAVOR TO ASK OF YOU?
A FAVOR? ME? WHATEVER COULD YOU WANT FROM LITTLE OL' ME?

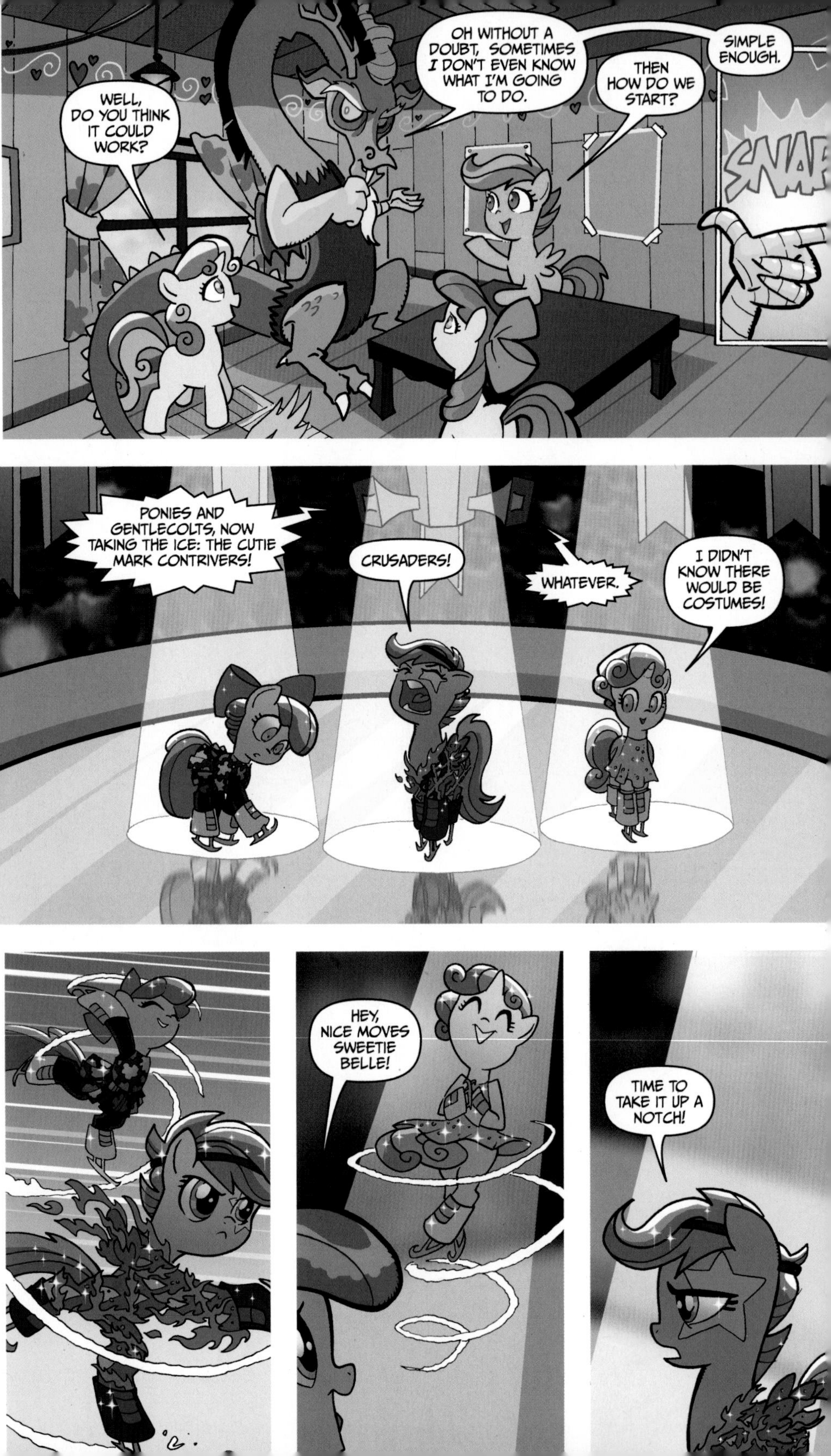
WELL, DO YOU THINK IT COULD WORK?
OH WITHOUT A DOUBT, SOMETIMES I DON'T EVEN KNOW WHAT I'M GOING TO DO.
THEN HOW DO WE START?
SIMPLE ENOUGH.
SNAP
PONIES AND GENTLECOLTS, NOW TAKING THE ICE: THE CUTIE MARK CONTRIVERS!
CRUSADERS!
WHATEVER.
I DIDN'T KNOW THERE WOULD BE COSTUMES!
HEY, NICE MOVES SWEETIE BELLE!
TIME TO TAKE IT UP A NOTCH!

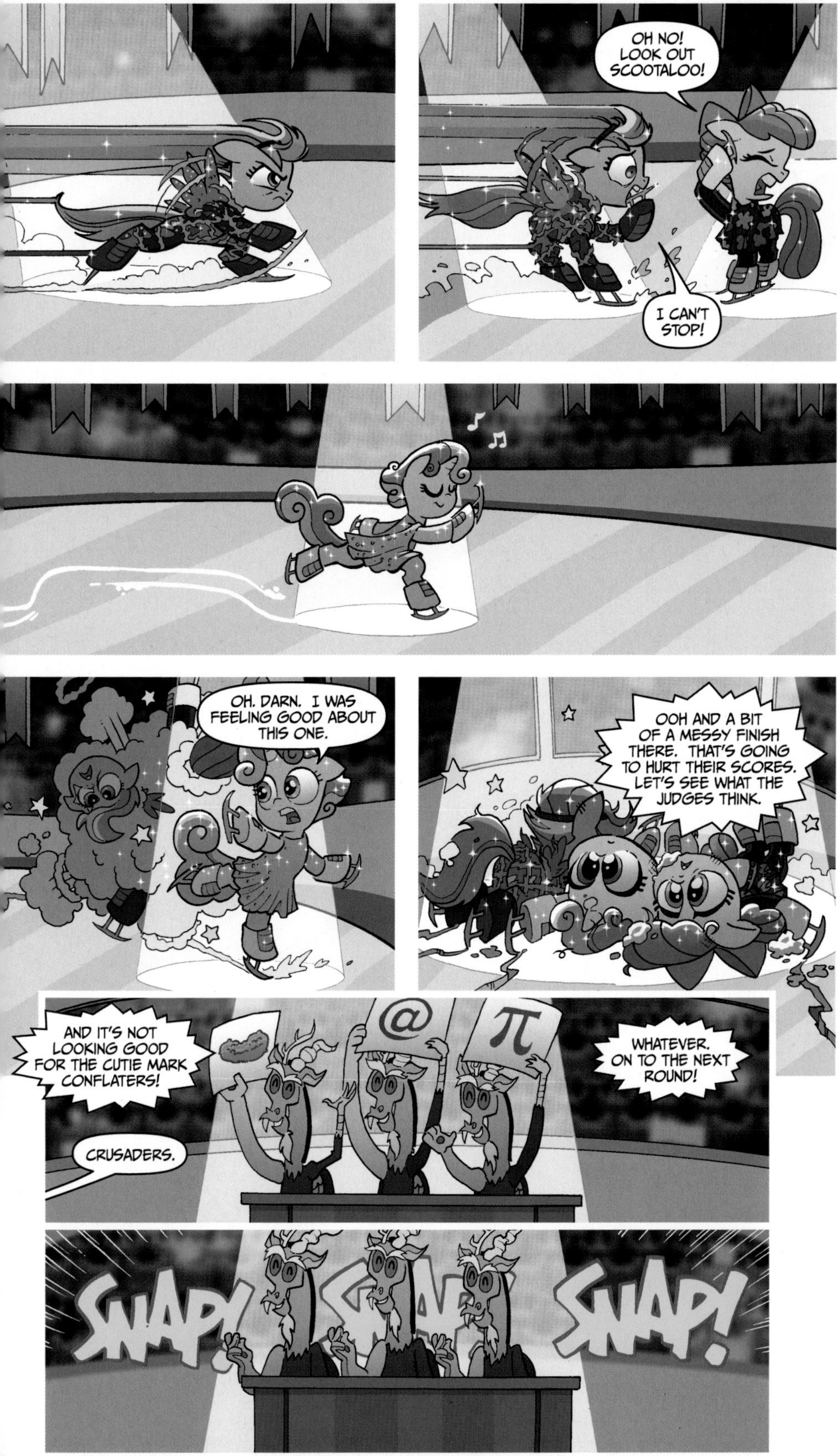
OH NO! LOOK OUT SCOOTALOO!
I CAN'T STOP!
OH. DARN. I WAS FEELING GOOD ABOUT THIS ONE.
OOH AND A BIT OF A MESSY FINISH THERE. THAT'S GOING TO HURT THEIR SCORES. LET'S SEE WHAT THE JUDGES THINK.
AND IT'S NOT LOOKING GOOD FOR THE CUTIE MARK CONFLATERS!
@
π
WHATEVER. ON TO THE NEXT ROUND!
CRUSADERS.
SNAP!
SNAP!
SNAP!

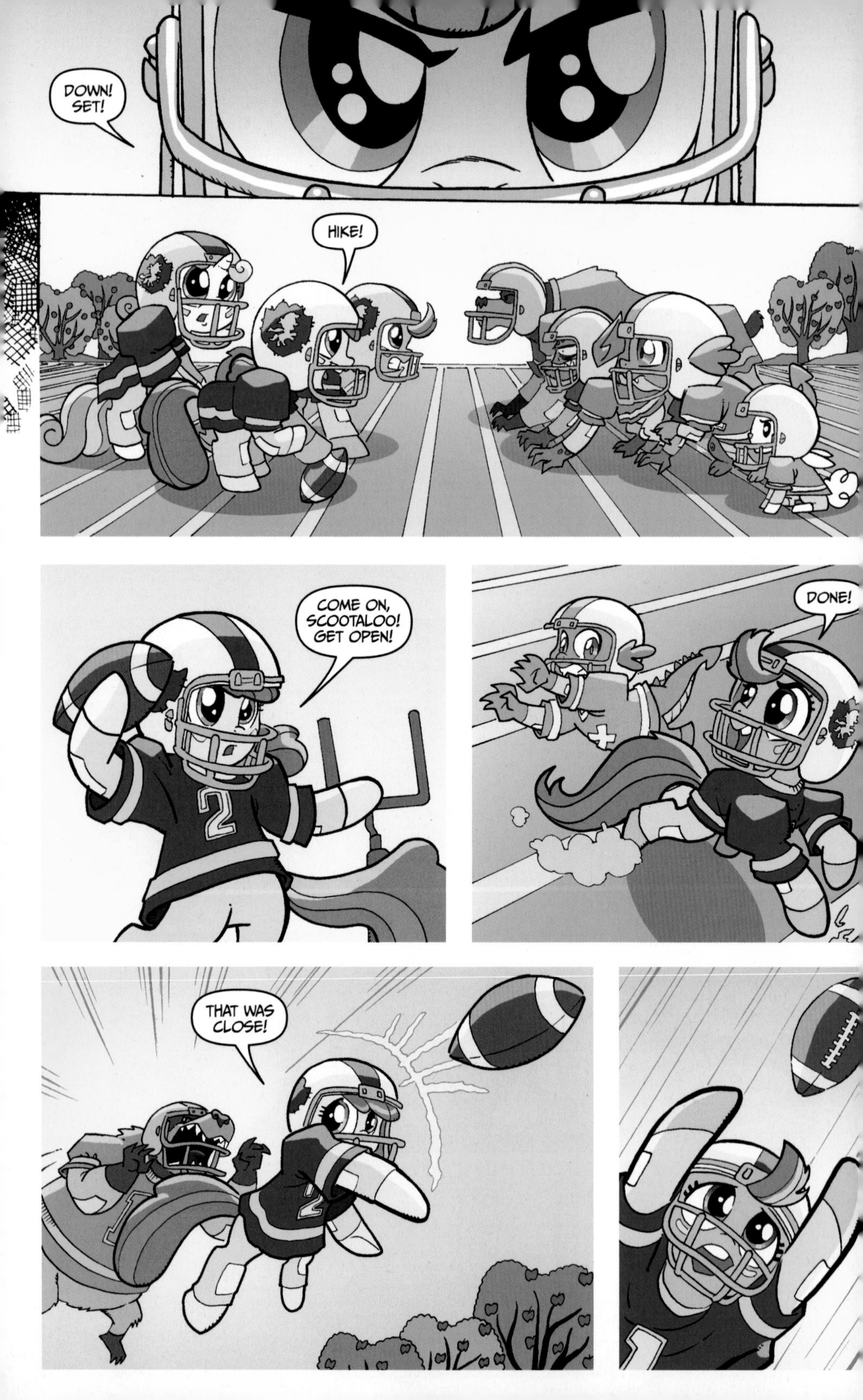
DOWN! SET!
HIKE!
COME ON, SCOOTALOO! GET OPEN!
DONE!
THAT WAS CLOSE!

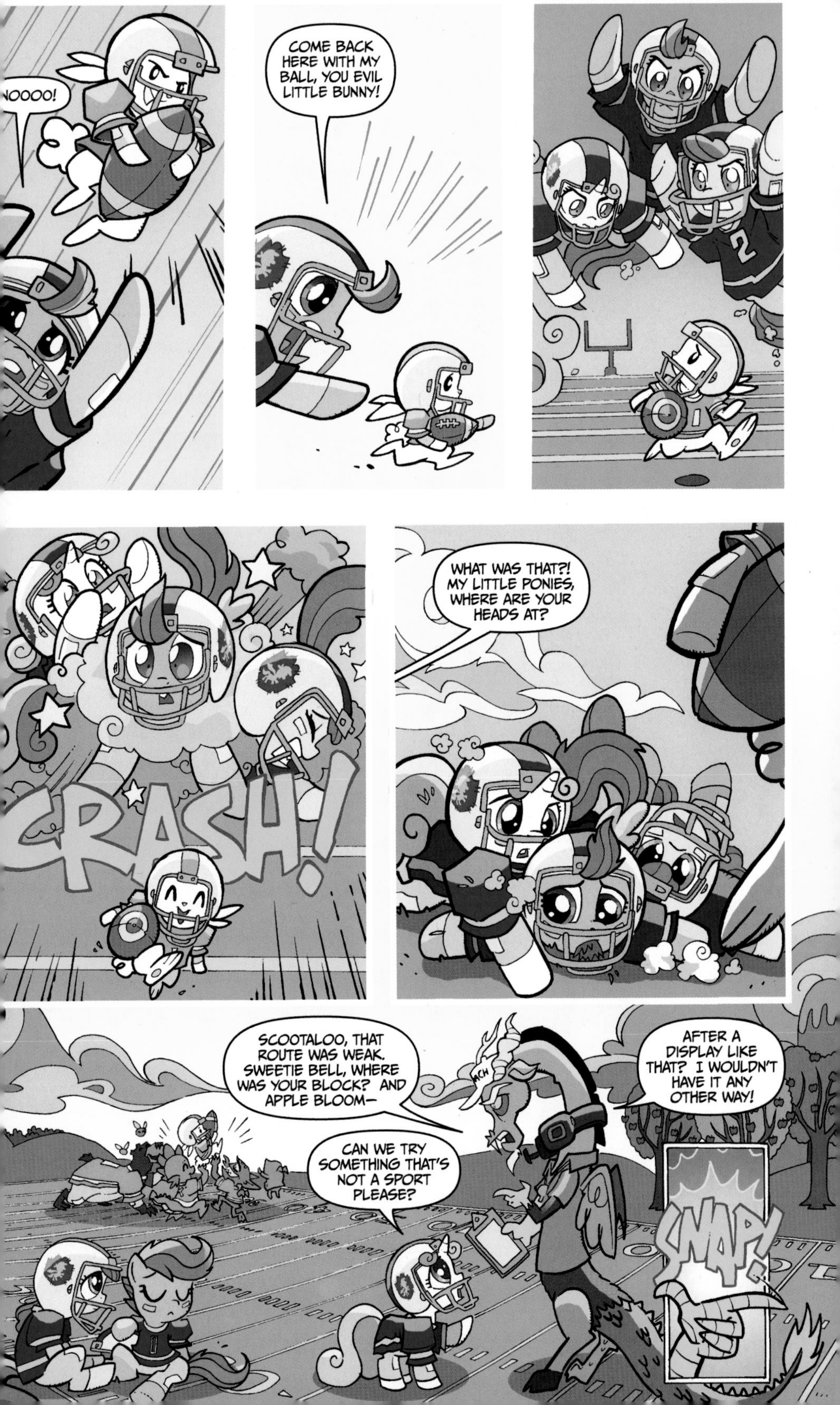
NOOOO!
COME BACK HERE WITH MY BALL, YOU EVIL LITTLE BUNNY!
CRASH!
WHAT WAS THAT?! MY LITTLE PONIES, WHERE ARE YOUR HEADS AT?
SCOOTALOO, THAT ROUTE WAS WEAK. SWEETIE BELL, WHERE WAS YOUR BLOCK? AND APPLE BLOOM—
CAN WE TRY SOMETHING THAT'S NOT A SPORT PLEASE?
AFTER A DISPLAY LIKE THAT? I WOULDN'T HAVE IT ANY OTHER WAY!
SNAP!

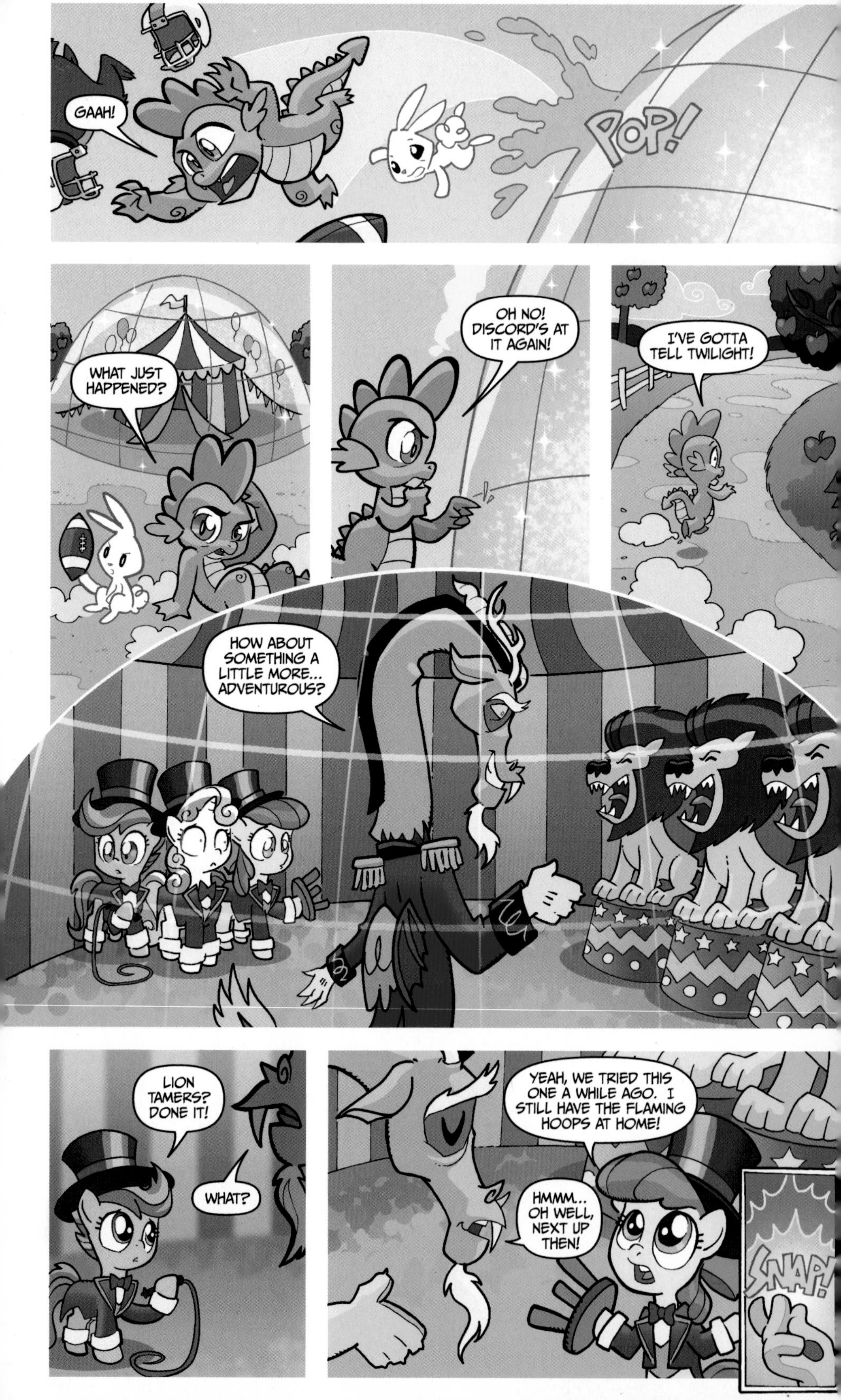
GAAH!
POP!
WHAT JUST HAPPENED?
OH NO! DISCORD'S AT IT AGAIN!
I'VE GOTTA TELL TWILIGHT!
HOW ABOUT SOMETHING A LITTLE MORE... ADVENTUROUS?
LION TAMERS? DONE IT!
WHAT?
YEAH, WE TRIED THIS ONE A WHILE AGO. I STILL HAVE THE FLAMING HOOPS AT HOME!
HMMM.. OH WELL, NEXT UP THEN!
SNAP!

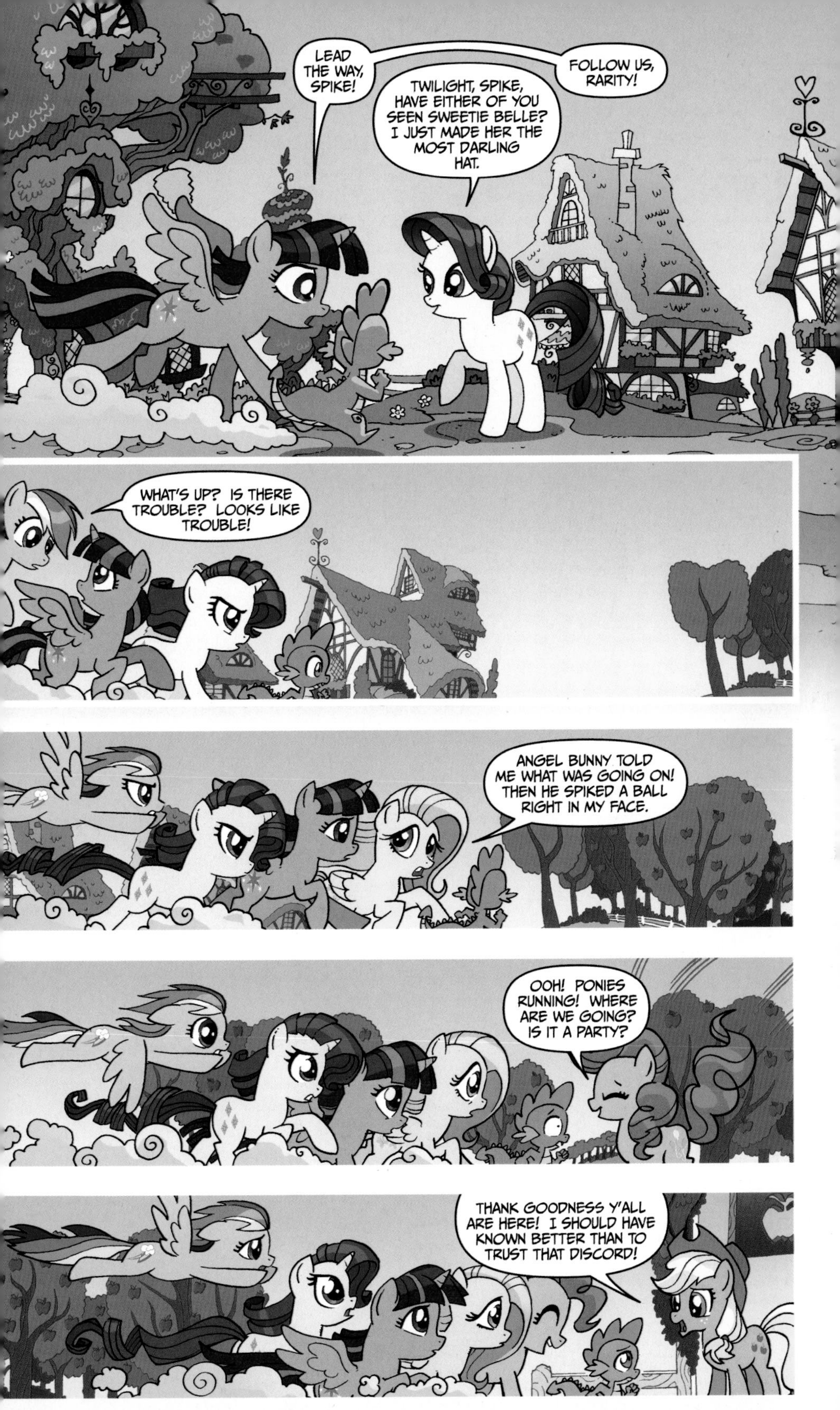
LEAD THE WAY, SPIKE!
FOLLOW US, RARITY!
TWILIGHT, SPIKE, HAVE EITHER OF YOU SEEN SWEETIE BELLE? I JUST MADE HER THE MOST DARLING HAT.
WHAT'S UP? IS THERE TROUBLE? LOOKS LIKE TROUBLE!
ANGEL BUNNY TOLD ME WHAT WAS GOING ON! THEN HE SPIKED A BALL RIGHT IN MY FACE.
OOH! PONIES RUNNING! WHERE ARE WE GOING? IS IT A PARTY?
THANK GOODNESS Y'ALL ARE HERE! I SHOULD HAVE KNOWN BETTER THAN TO TRUST THAT DISCORD!

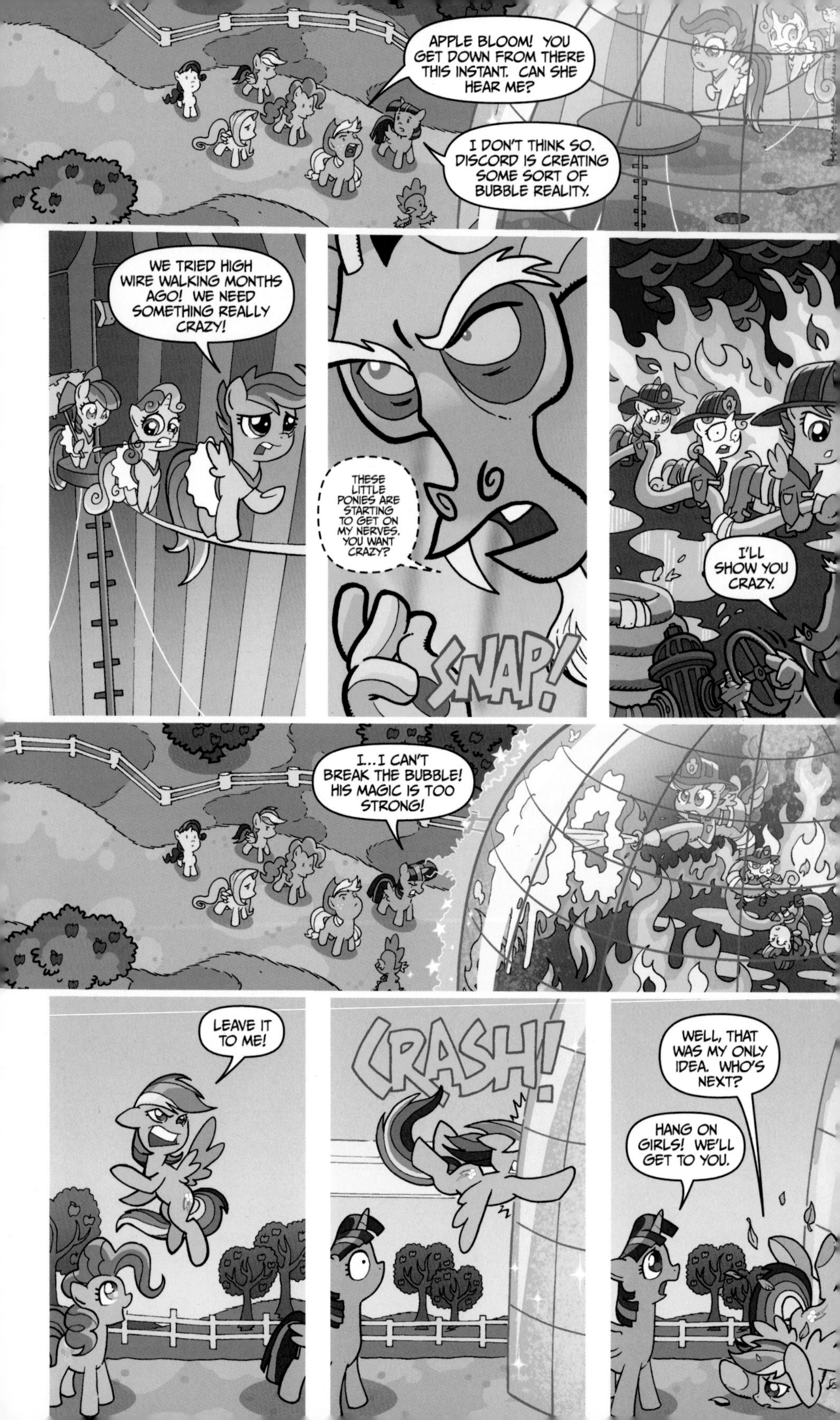
APPLE BLOOM! YOU GET DOWN FROM THERE THIS INSTANT. CAN SHE HEAR ME?
I DON'T THINK SO. DISCORD IS CREATING SOME SORT OF BUBBLE REALITY.
WE TRIED HIGH WIRE WALKING MONTHS AGO! WE NEED SOMETHING REALLY CRAZY!
THESE LITTLE PONIES ARE STARTING TO GET ON MY NERVES. YOU WANT CRAZY?
SNAP!
I'LL SHOW YOU CRAZY.
I...I CAN'T BREAK THE BUBBLE! HIS MAGIC IS TOO STRONG!
LEAVE IT TO ME!
CRASH!
WELL, THAT WAS MY ONLY IDEA. WHO'S NEXT?
HANG ON GIRLS! WE'LL GET TO YOU.

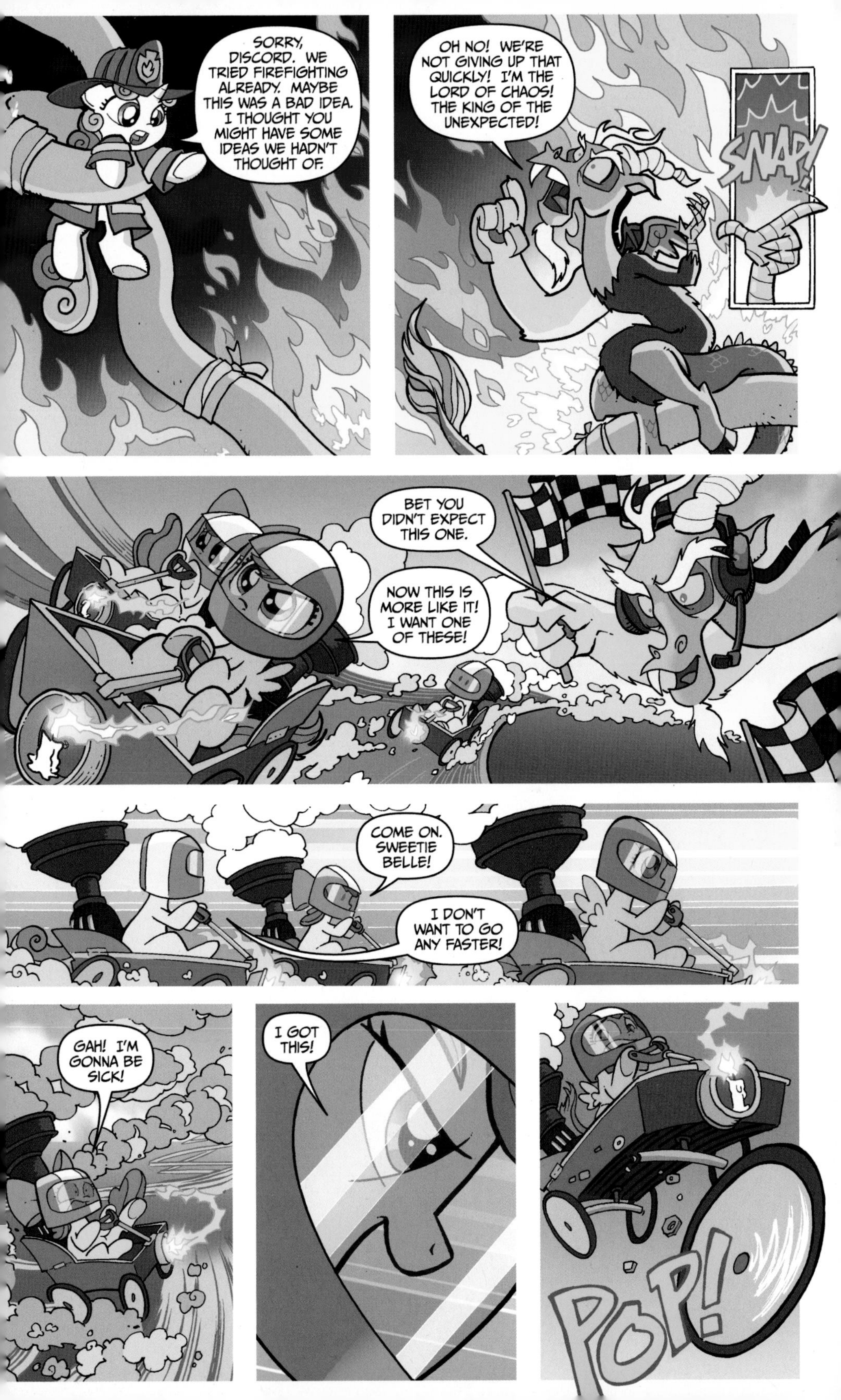
SORRY, DISCORD. WE TRIED FIREFIGHTING ALREADY. MAYBE THIS WAS A BAD IDEA. I THOUGHT YOU MIGHT HAVE SOME IDEAS WE HADN'T THOUGHT OF.
OH NO! WE'RE NOT GIVING UP THAT QUICKLY! I'M THE LORD OF CHAOS! THE KING OF THE UNEXPECTED!
SNAP!
BET YOU DIDN'T EXPECT THIS ONE.
NOW THIS IS MORE LIKE IT! I WANT ONE OF THESE!
COME ON. SWEETIE BELLE!
I DON'T WANT TO GO ANY FASTER!
GAH! I'M GONNA BE SICK!
I GOT THIS!
POP!

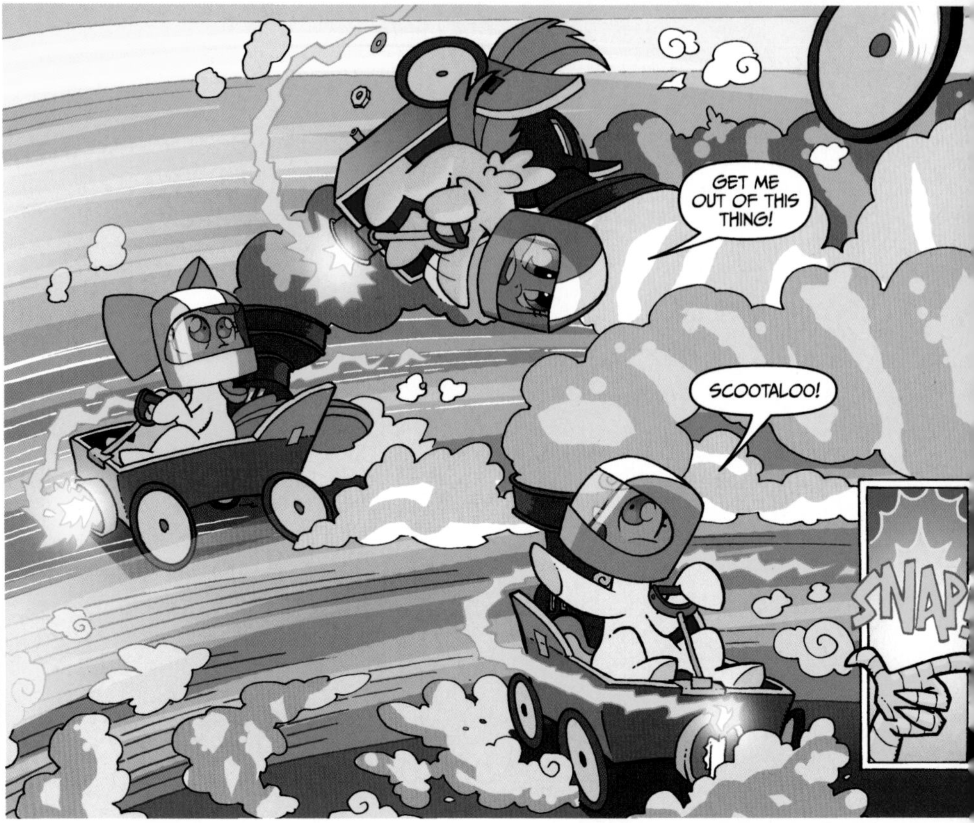
GET ME OUT OF THIS THING!
SCOOTALOO!
SNAP!

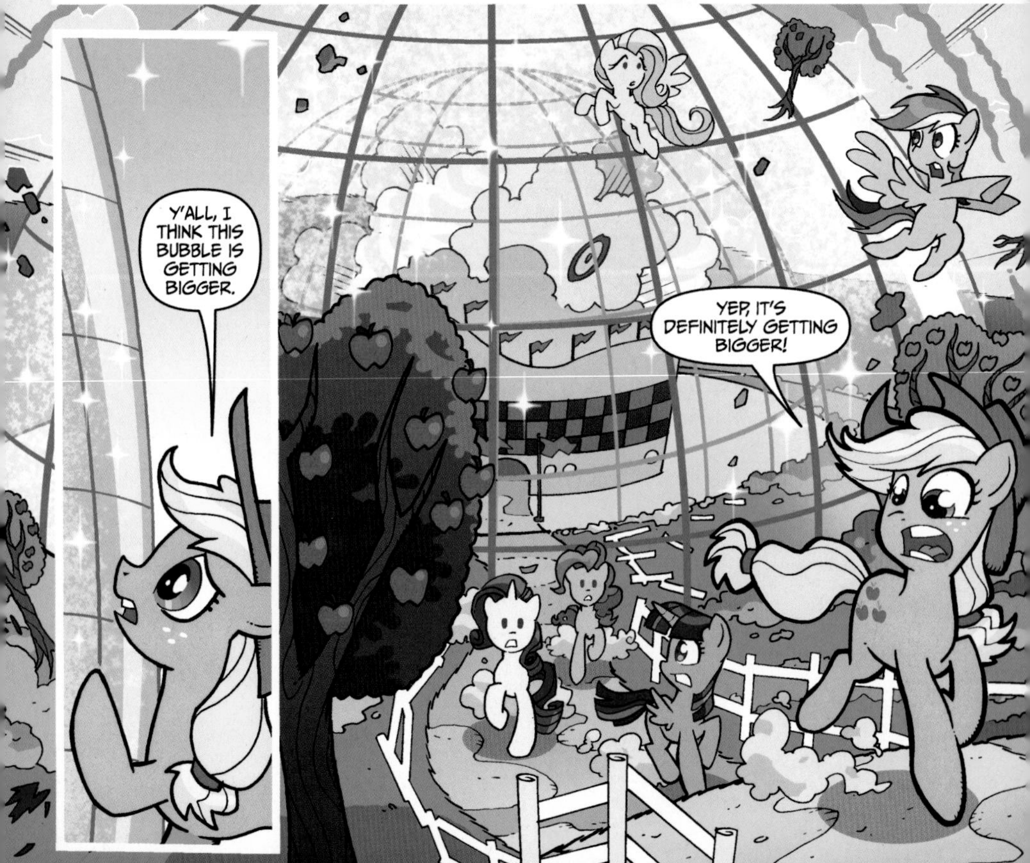
Y'ALL, I THINK THIS BUBBLE IS GETTING BIGGER.
YEP, IT'S DEFINITELY GETTING BIGGER!

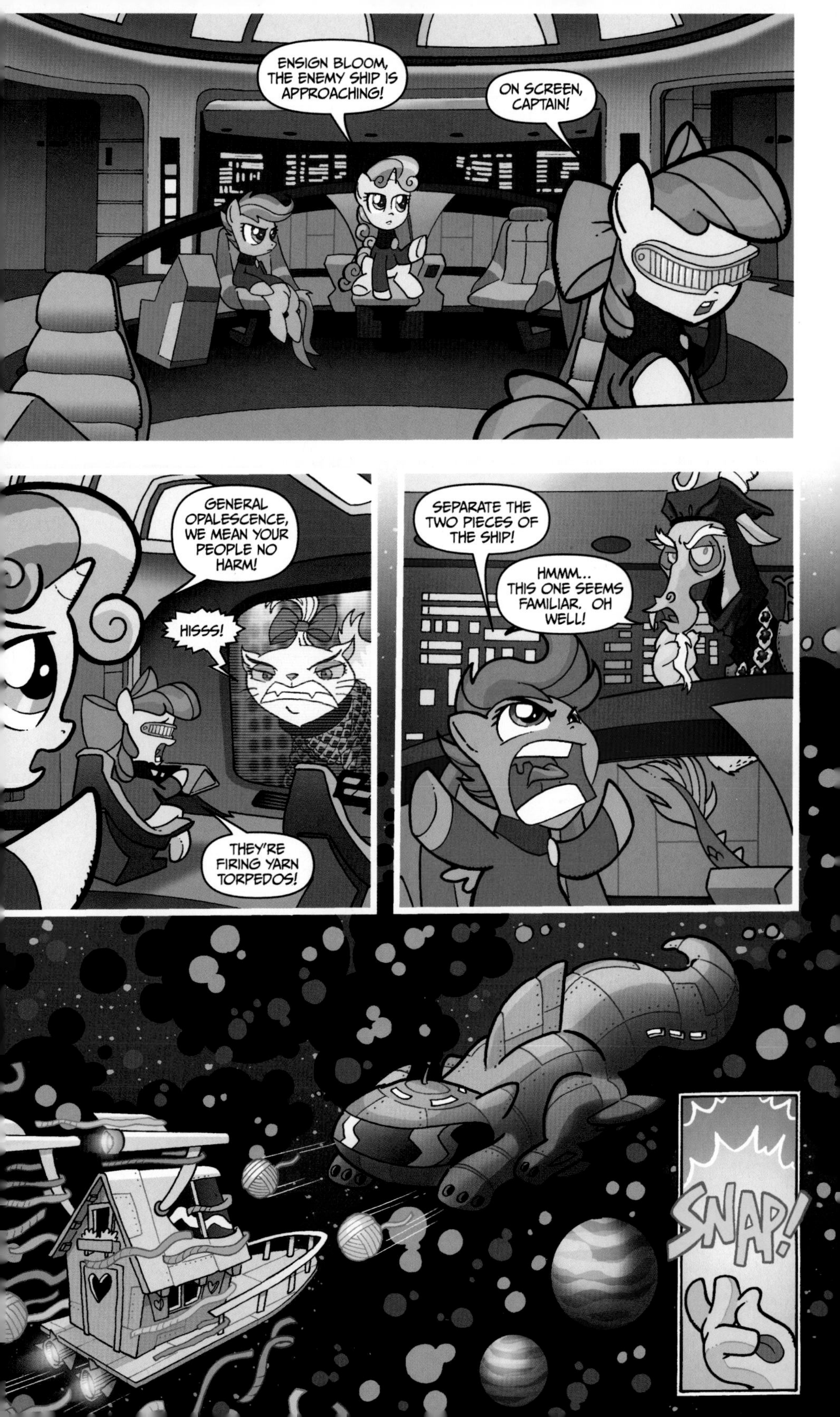
ENSIGN BLOOM, THE ENEMY SHIP IS APPROACHING!
ON SCREEN, CAPTAIN!
GENERAL OPALESCENCE, WE MEAN YOUR PEOPLE NO HARM!
HISSS!
THEY'RE FIRING YARN TORPEDOS!
SEPARATE THE TWO PIECES OF THE SHIP!
HMMM... THIS ONE SEEMS FAMILIAR. OH WELL!
SNAP!

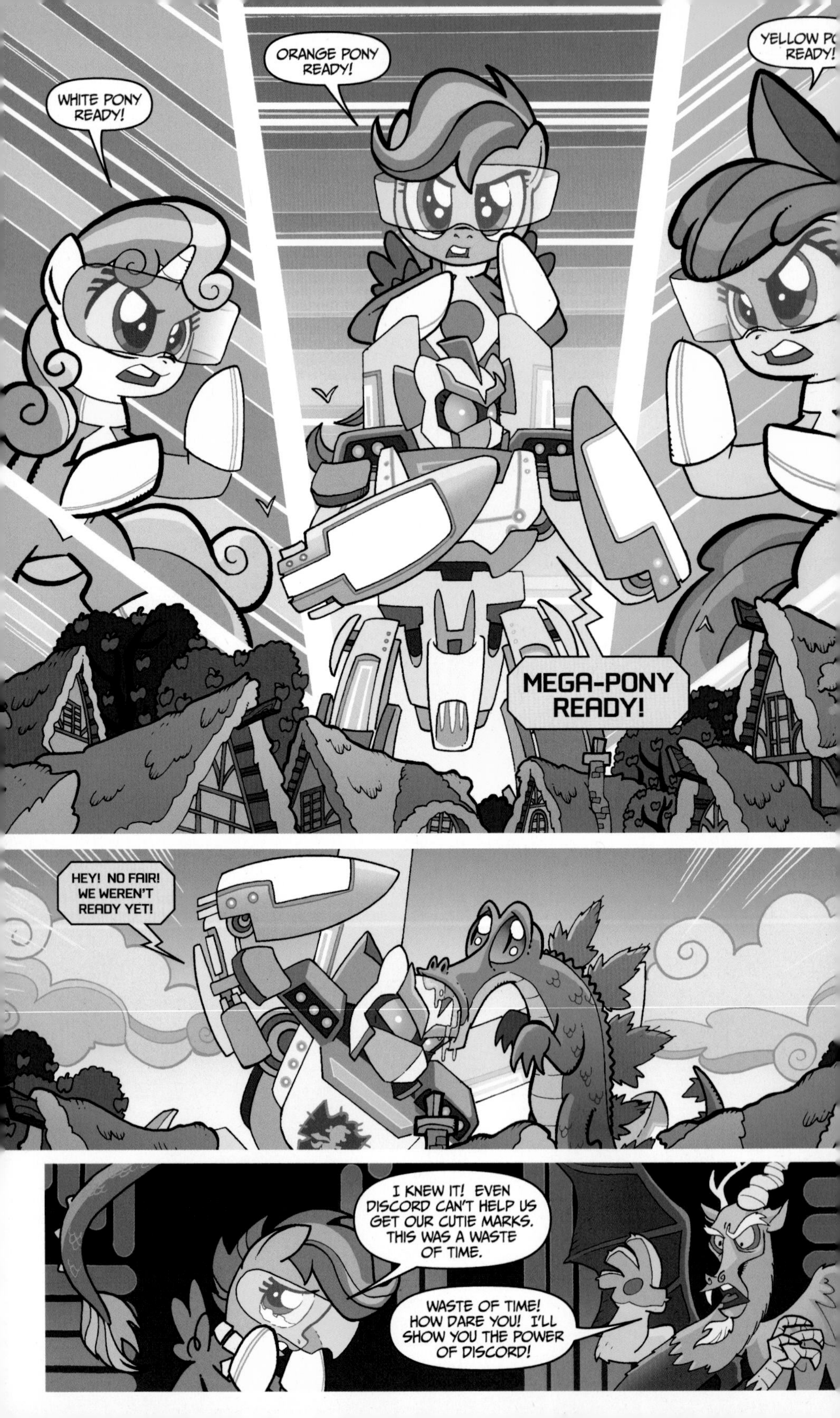
WHITE PONY READY!
ORANGE PONY READY!
YELLOW PO READY!
MEGA-PONY READY!
HEY! NO FAIR! WE WEREN'T READY YET!
I KNEW IT! EVEN DISCORD CAN'T HELP US GET OUR CUTIE MARKS. THIS WAS A WASTE OF TIME.
WASTE OF TIME! HOW DARE YOU! I'LL SHOW YOU THE POWER OF DISCORD!

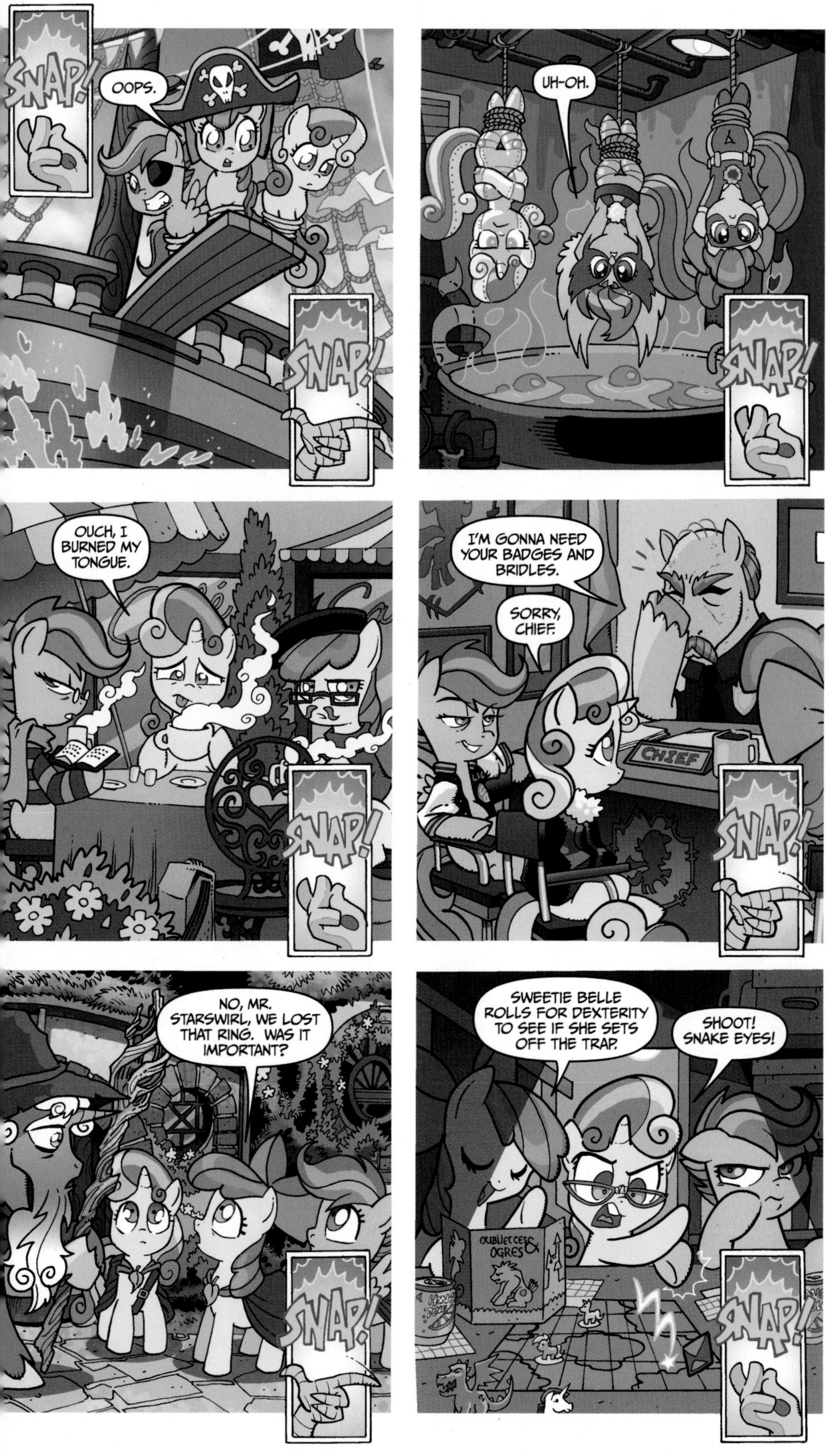
SNAP!
OOPS.
SNAP!
UH-OH.
SNAP!
OUCH, I BURNED MY TONGUE.
SNAP!
I'M GONNA NEED YOUR BADGES AND BRIDLES.
SORRY, CHIEF.
CHIEF
SNAP!
NO, MR. STARSWIRL, WE LOST THAT RING. WAS IT IMPORTANT?
SNAP!
SWEETIE BELLE ROLLS FOR DEXTERITY TO SEE IF SHE SETS OFF THE TRAP.
SHOOT! SNAKE EYES!
OUBLIETTES & OGRES
SNAP!

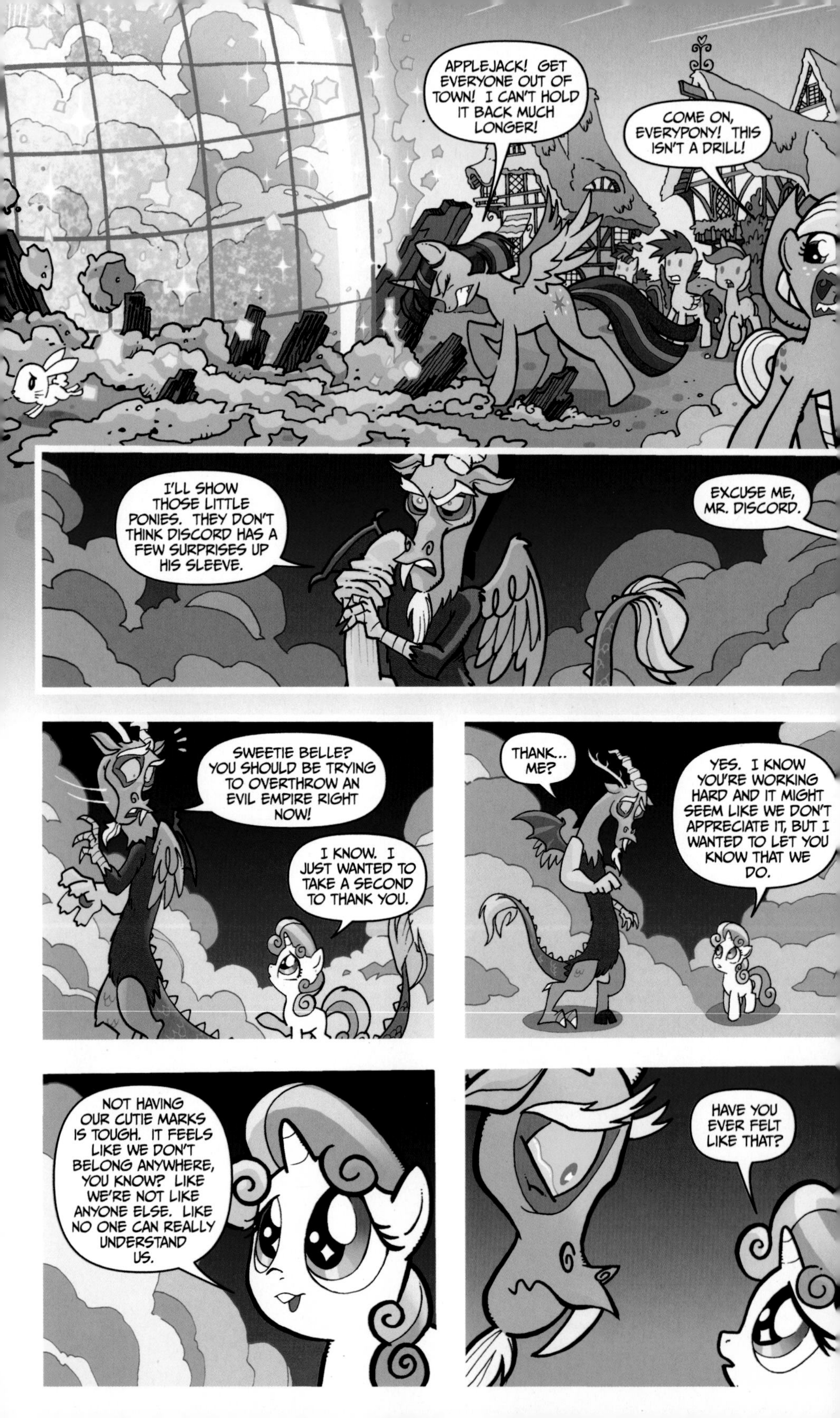
APPLEJACK! GET EVERYONE OUT OF TOWN! I CAN'T HOLD IT BACK MUCH LONGER!
COME ON, EVERYPONY! THIS ISN'T A DRILL!
I'LL SHOW THOSE LITTLE PONIES. THEY DON'T THINK DISCORD HAS A FEW SURPRISES UP HIS SLEEVE.
EXCUSE ME, MR. DISCORD.
SWEETIE BELLE? YOU SHOULD BE TRYING TO OVERTHROW AN EVIL EMPIRE RIGHT NOW!
I KNOW. I JUST WANTED TO TAKE A SECOND TO THANK YOU.
THANK... ME?
YES. I KNOW YOU'RE WORKING HARD AND IT MIGHT SEEM LIKE WE DON'T APPRECIATE IT, BUT I WANTED TO LET YOU KNOW THAT WE DO.
NOT HAVING OUR CUTIE MARKS IS TOUGH. IT FEELS LIKE WE DON'T BELONG ANYWHERE, YOU KNOW? LIKE WE'RE NOT LIKE ANYONE ELSE. LIKE NO ONE CAN REALLY UNDERSTAND US.
HAVE YOU EVER FELT LIKE THAT?

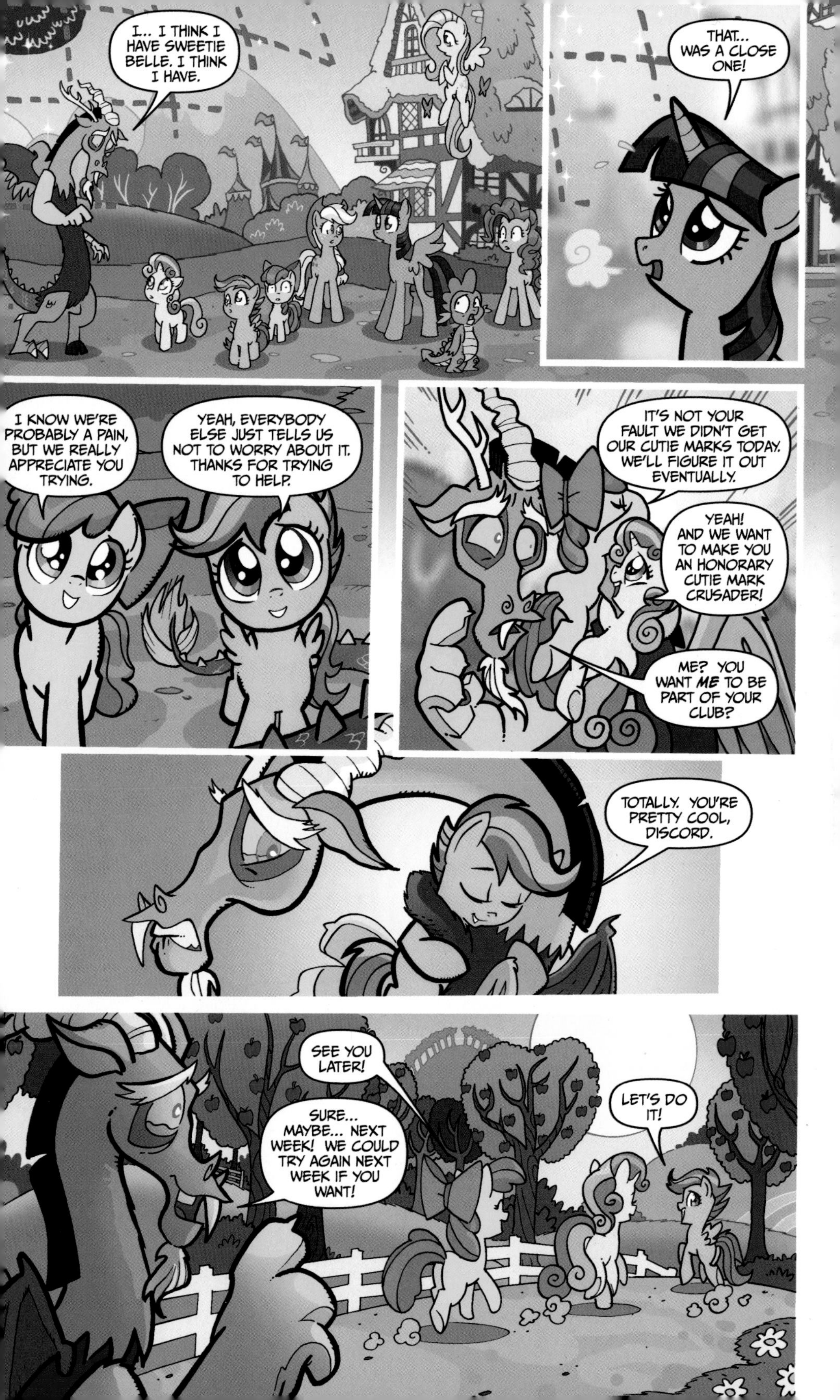

I... I THINK I HAVE SWEETIE BELLE. I THINK I HAVE.
THAT... WAS A CLOSE ONE!
I KNOW WE'RE PROBABLY A PAIN, BUT WE REALLY APPRECIATE YOU TRYING.
YEAH, EVERYBODY ELSE JUST TELLS US NOT TO WORRY ABOUT IT. THANKS FOR TRYING TO HELP.
IT'S NOT YOUR FAULT WE DIDN'T GET OUR CUTIE MARKS TODAY. WE'LL FIGURE IT OUT EVENTUALLY.
YEAH! AND WE WANT TO MAKE YOU AN HONORARY CUTIE MARK CRUSADER!
ME? YOU WANT **ME** TO BE PART OF YOUR CLUB?
TOTALLY. YOU'RE PRETTY COOL, DISCORD.
SEE YOU LATER!
SURE... MAYBE... NEXT WEEK! WE COULD TRY AGAIN NEXT WEEK IF YOU WANT!
LET'S DO IT!

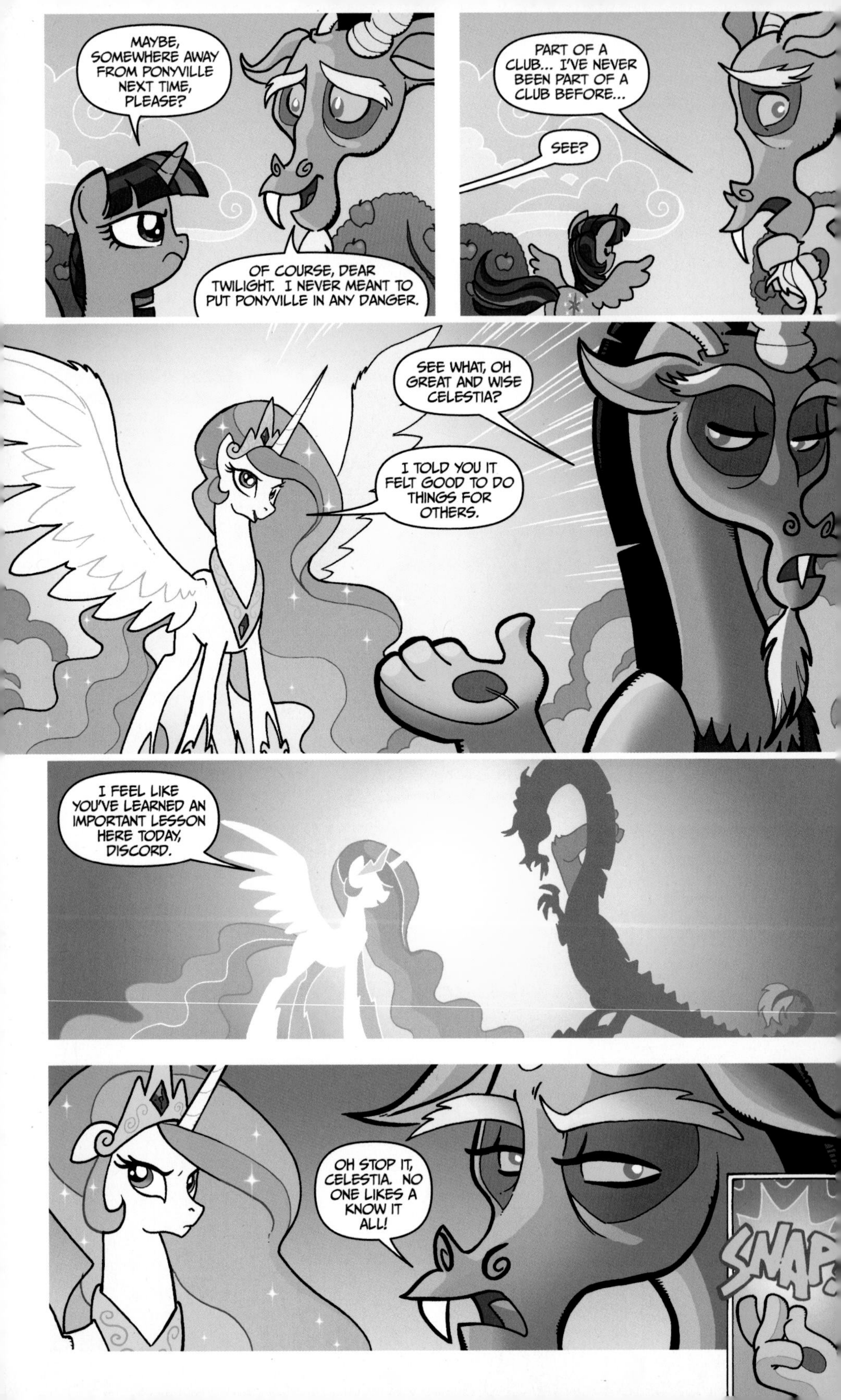
MAYBE, SOMEWHERE AWAY FROM PONYVILLE NEXT TIME, PLEASE?
OF COURSE, DEAR TWILIGHT. I NEVER MEANT TO PUT PONYVILLE IN ANY DANGER.
PART OF A CLUB... I'VE NEVER BEEN PART OF A CLUB BEFORE...
SEE?
SEE WHAT, OH GREAT AND WISE CELESTIA?
I TOLD YOU IT FELT GOOD TO DO THINGS FOR OTHERS.
I FEEL LIKE YOU'VE LEARNED AN IMPORTANT LESSON HERE TODAY, DISCORD.
OH STOP IT, CELESTIA. NO ONE LIKES A KNOW IT ALL!
SNAP!

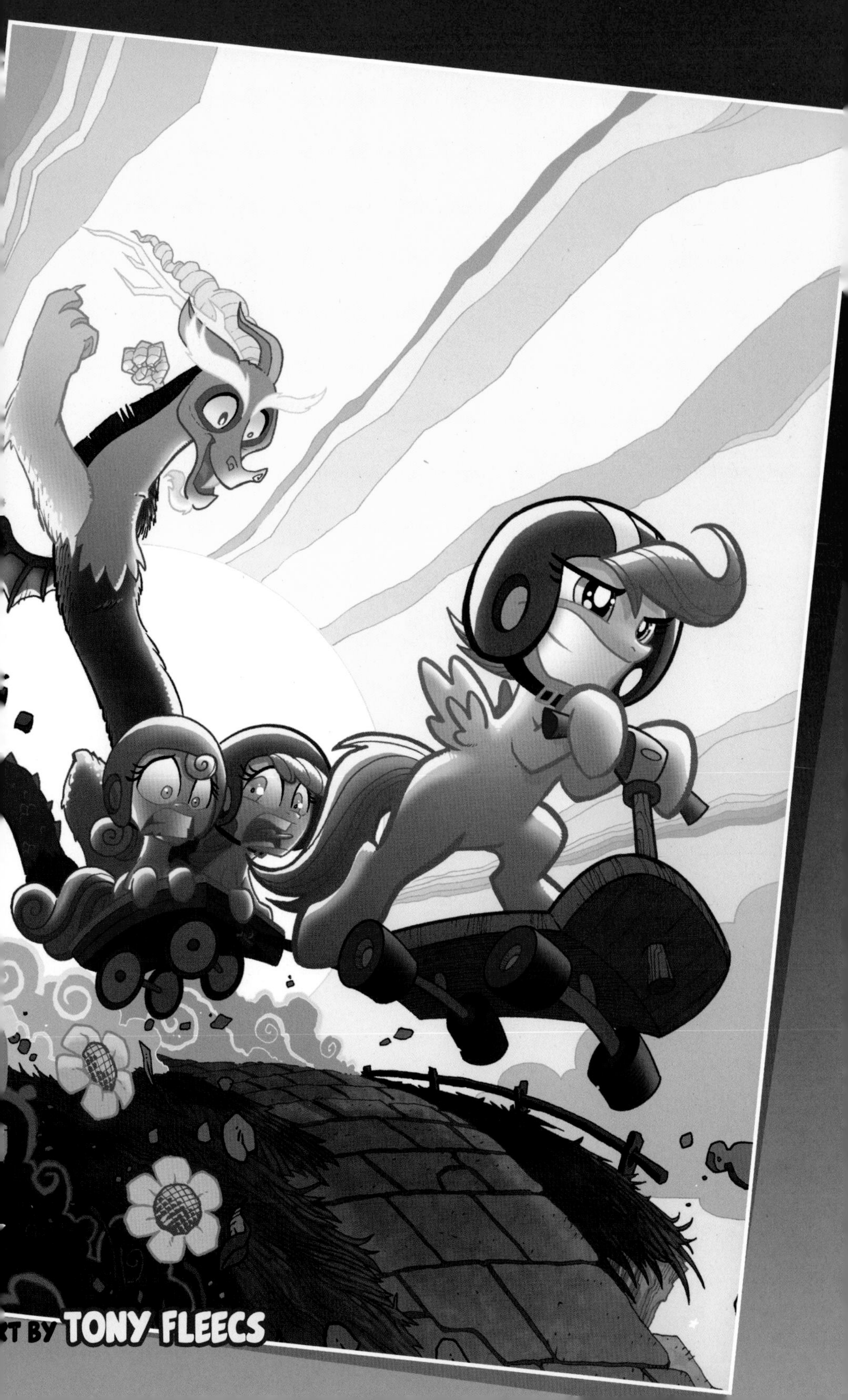
RT BY TONY FLEECS

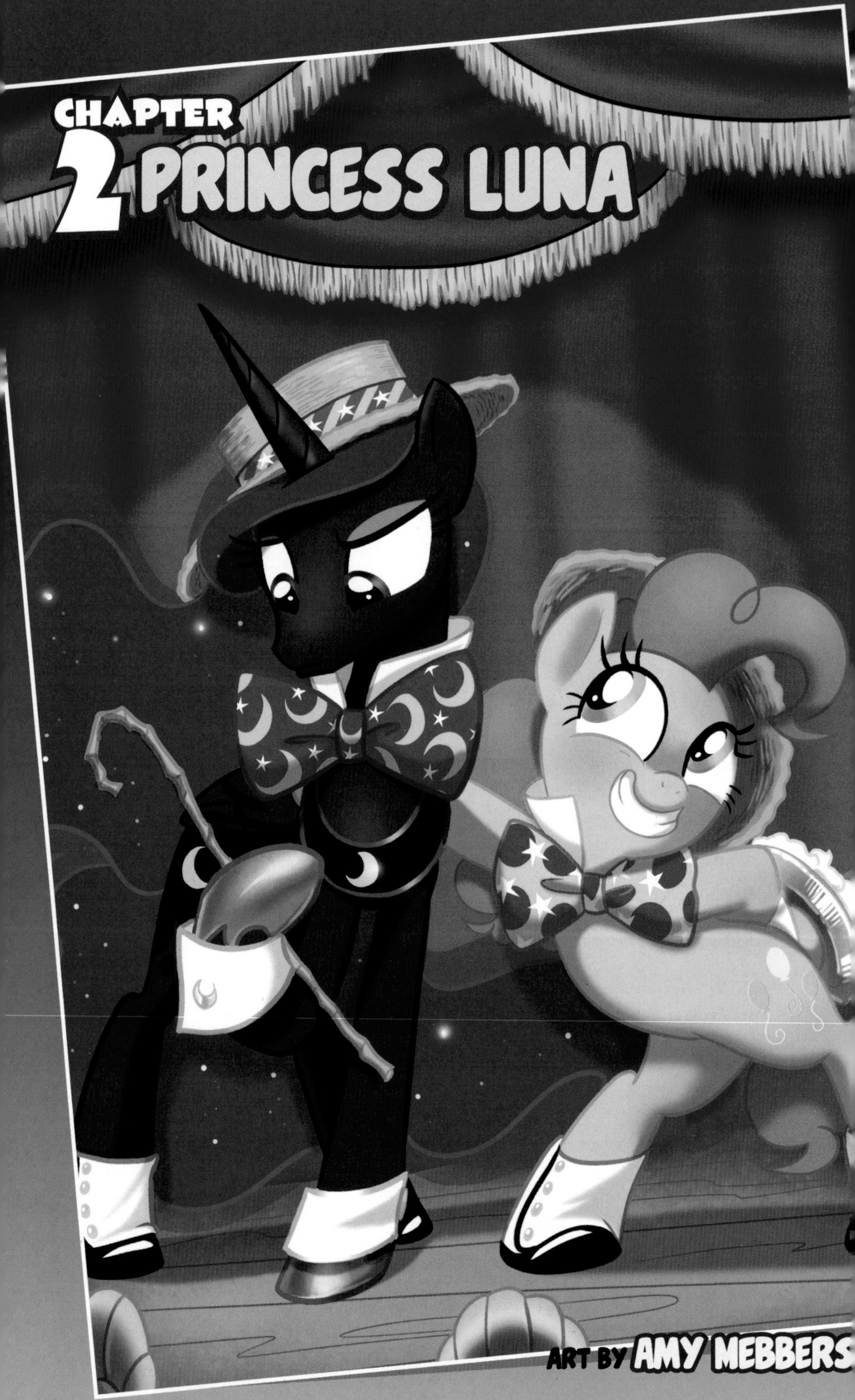
CHAPTER 2 PRINCESS LUNA
ART BY AMY MEBBERS

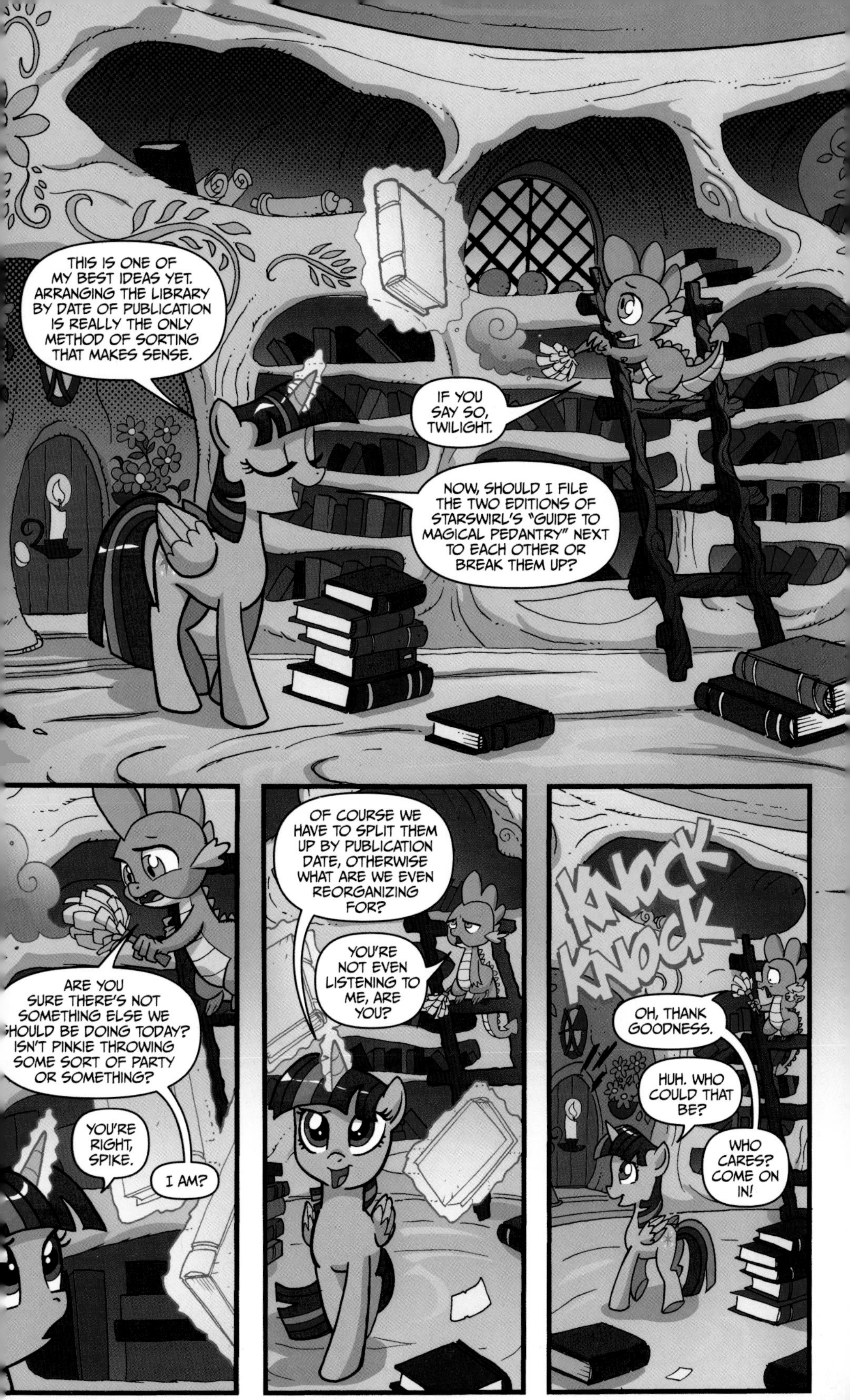
THIS IS ONE OF MY BEST IDEAS YET. ARRANGING THE LIBRARY BY DATE OF PUBLICATION IS REALLY THE ONLY METHOD OF SORTING THAT MAKES SENSE.
IF YOU SAY SO, TWILIGHT.
NOW, SHOULD I FILE THE TWO EDITIONS OF STARSWIRL'S "GUIDE TO MAGICAL PEDANTRY" NEXT TO EACH OTHER OR BREAK THEM UP?
ARE YOU SURE THERE'S NOT SOMETHING ELSE WE SHOULD BE DOING TODAY? ISN'T PINKIE THROWING SOME SORT OF PARTY OR SOMETHING?
YOU'RE RIGHT, SPIKE.
I AM?
OF COURSE WE HAVE TO SPLIT THEM UP BY PUBLICATION DATE, OTHERWISE WHAT ARE WE EVEN REORGANIZING FOR?
YOU'RE NOT EVEN LISTENING TO ME, ARE YOU?
KNOCK KNOCK
OH, THANK GOODNESS.
HUH. WHO COULD THAT BE?
WHO CARES? COME ON IN!

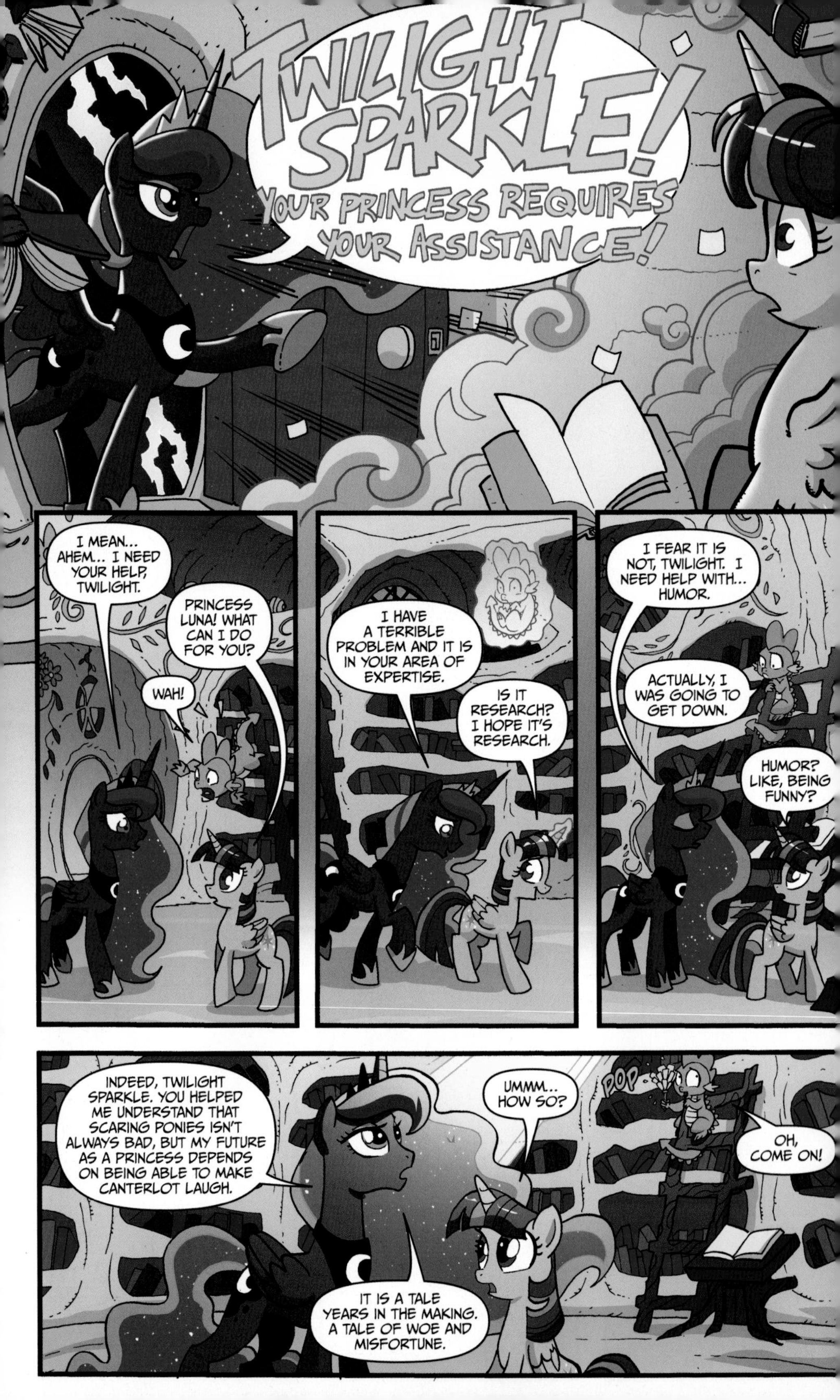
TWILIGHT SPARKLE! YOUR PRINCESS REQUIRES YOUR ASSISTANCE!
I MEAN... AHEM... I NEED YOUR HELP, TWILIGHT.
PRINCESS LUNA! WHAT CAN I DO FOR YOU?
WAH!
I HAVE A TERRIBLE PROBLEM AND IT IS IN YOUR AREA OF EXPERTISE.
IS IT RESEARCH? I HOPE IT'S RESEARCH.
I FEAR IT IS NOT, TWILIGHT. I NEED HELP WITH... HUMOR.
ACTUALLY, I WAS GOING TO GET DOWN.
HUMOR? LIKE, BEING FUNNY?
INDEED, TWILIGHT SPARKLE. YOU HELPED ME UNDERSTAND THAT SCARING PONIES ISN'T ALWAYS BAD, BUT MY FUTURE AS A PRINCESS DEPENDS ON BEING ABLE TO MAKE CANTERLOT LAUGH.
UMMM.. HOW SO?
POP
OH, COME ON!
IT IS A TALE YEARS IN THE MAKING. A TALE OF WOE AND MISFORTUNE.

YEARS, MY SISTER AND I LIVED [AP]RT FROM THE COMMON PONIES [E]QUESTRIA. WE PROTECTED [THE]M AND MADE THE DAY AND THE [NIGH]T. WE WERE SEEN AS MORE [THA]N MERE PONIES.

[TH]EN, AS YOU KNOW, I CHANGED. [I] DROVE MY PEOPLE AWAY AND [F]RIGHTENED THEM TERRIBLY.

MY SISTER, TERRIFIED BY WHAT HAD HAPPENED TO ME, DECIDED TO BRING HERSELF CLOSER TO THE AVERAGE PONY. THE GRANDEST CHANGE SHE MADE WAS TO HOLD A BANQUET.

SHE CALLED IT "CHUCKLE-LOT." IT WAS A CHANCE FOR CELESTIA TO CUT LOOSE. THE OTHER PONIES WOULD GET TO SEE THAT SHE WASN'T ALWAYS SERIOUS.

[O]NCE I RETURNED, SHE INVITED [M]E TO TAKE PART AS WELL. I [F]EAR IT HAS NOT GONE WELL. [I] DO NOT KNOW HOW TO MAKE [P]ONIES LAUGH. MY SUBJECTS... [M]Y FELLOW PONIES ARE STILL [AF]RAID OF ME.

BUT THIS YEAR WILL BE DIFFERENT, TWILIGHT! I WANT TO MAKE THEM LIKE ME. I WANT TO BE FUNNY.

AND YOU WANT ME TO TEACH YOU?

INDEED! WHENEVER YOU AND YOUR FRIENDS VISIT YOU ARE ALWAYS LAUGHING AND LIGHTHEARTED. I WISH TO BE MORE LIKE THAT. CAN YOU TEACH ME?

OF COURSE I CAN! PRINCESS LUNA, YOU ARE GOING TO BE THE TOAST OF THIS YEAR'S CHUCKLE-LOT!

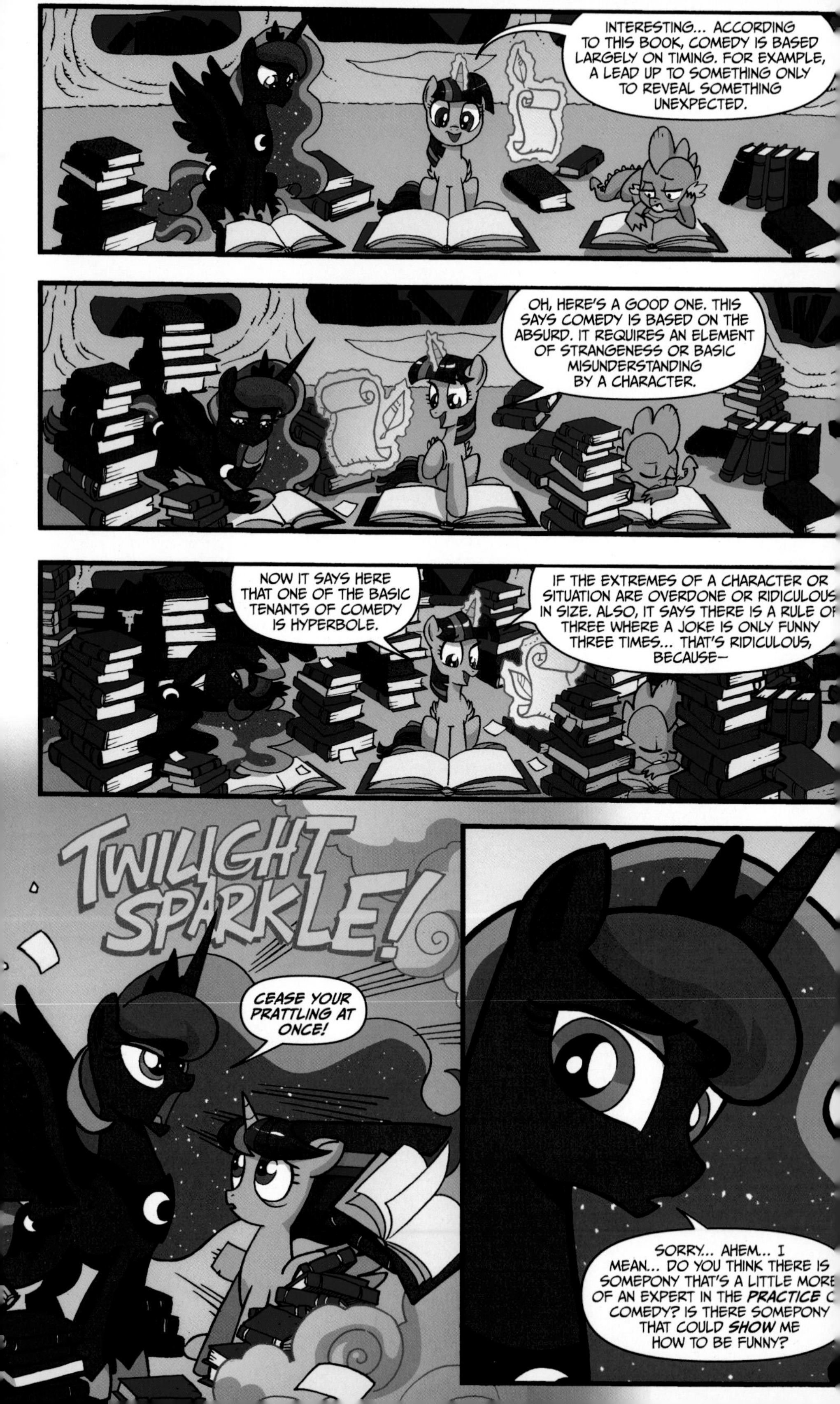
INTERESTING... ACCORDING TO THIS BOOK, COMEDY IS BASED LARGELY ON TIMING. FOR EXAMPLE, A LEAD UP TO SOMETHING ONLY TO REVEAL SOMETHING UNEXPECTED.
OH, HERE'S A GOOD ONE. THIS SAYS COMEDY IS BASED ON THE ABSURD. IT REQUIRES AN ELEMENT OF STRANGENESS OR BASIC MISUNDERSTANDING BY A CHARACTER.
NOW IT SAYS HERE THAT ONE OF THE BASIC TENANTS OF COMEDY IS HYPERBOLE.
IF THE EXTREMES OF A CHARACTER OR SITUATION ARE OVERDONE OR RIDICULOUS IN SIZE. ALSO, IT SAYS THERE IS A RULE OF THREE WHERE A JOKE IS ONLY FUNNY THREE TIMES... THAT'S RIDICULOUS, BECAUSE–
TWILIGHT SPARKLE!
CEASE YOUR PRATTLING AT ONCE!
SORRY... AHEM... I MEAN... DO YOU THINK THERE IS SOMEPONY THAT'S A LITTLE MORE OF AN EXPERT IN THE *PRACTICE* OF COMEDY? IS THERE SOMEPONY THAT COULD *SHOW* ME HOW TO BE FUNNY?

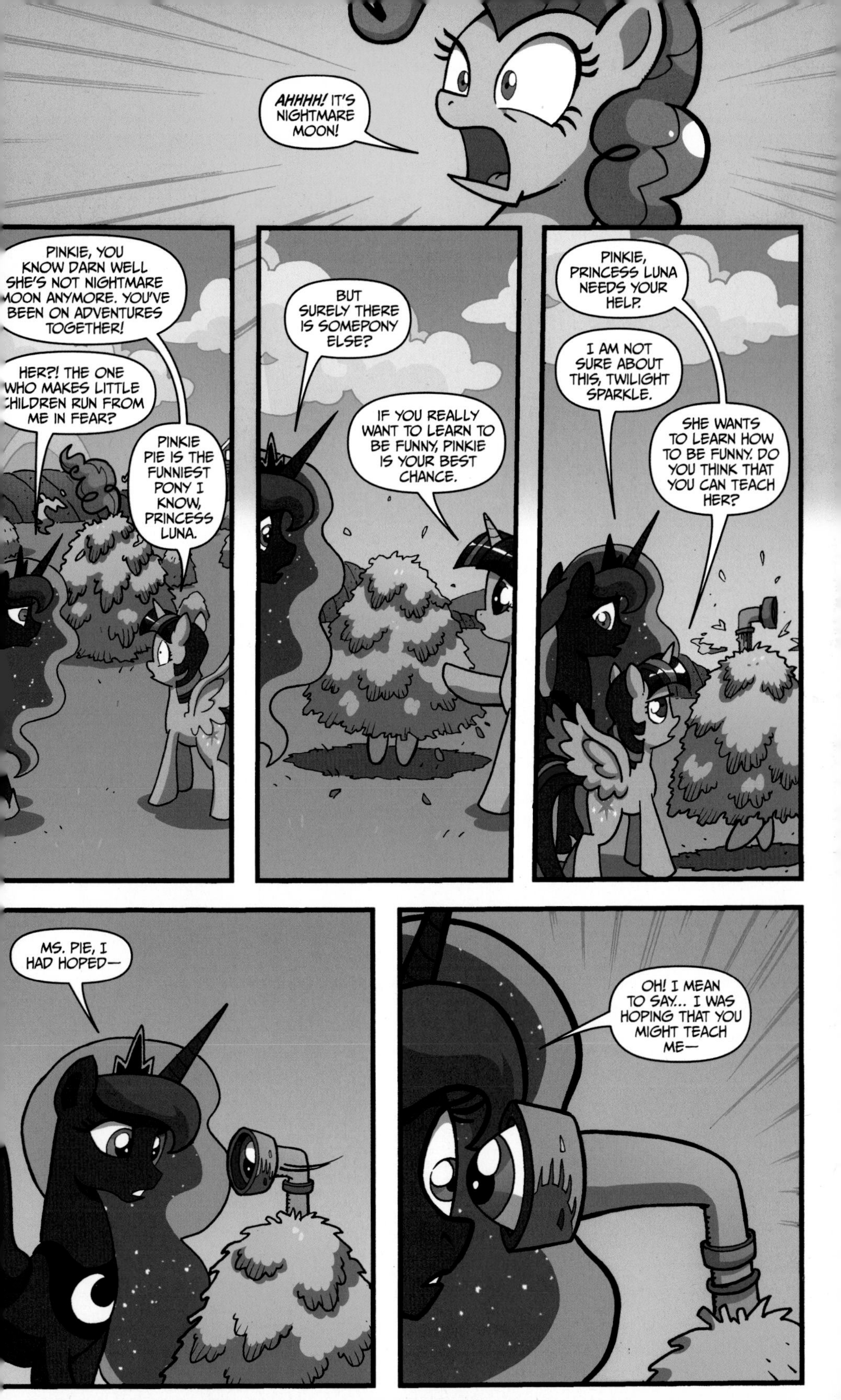
AHHHH! IT'S NIGHTMARE MOON!
PINKIE, YOU KNOW DARN WELL SHE'S NOT NIGHTMARE MOON ANYMORE. YOU'VE BEEN ON ADVENTURES TOGETHER!
HER?! THE ONE WHO MAKES LITTLE CHILDREN RUN FROM ME IN FEAR?
PINKIE PIE IS THE FUNNIEST PONY I KNOW, PRINCESS LUNA.
BUT SURELY THERE IS SOMEPONY ELSE?
IF YOU REALLY WANT TO LEARN TO BE FUNNY, PINKIE IS YOUR BEST CHANCE.
PINKIE, PRINCESS LUNA NEEDS YOUR HELP.
I AM NOT SURE ABOUT THIS, TWILIGHT SPARKLE.
SHE WANTS TO LEARN HOW TO BE FUNNY. DO YOU THINK THAT YOU CAN TEACH HER?
MS. PIE, I HAD HOPED—
OH! I MEAN TO SAY... I WAS HOPING THAT YOU MIGHT TEACH ME—

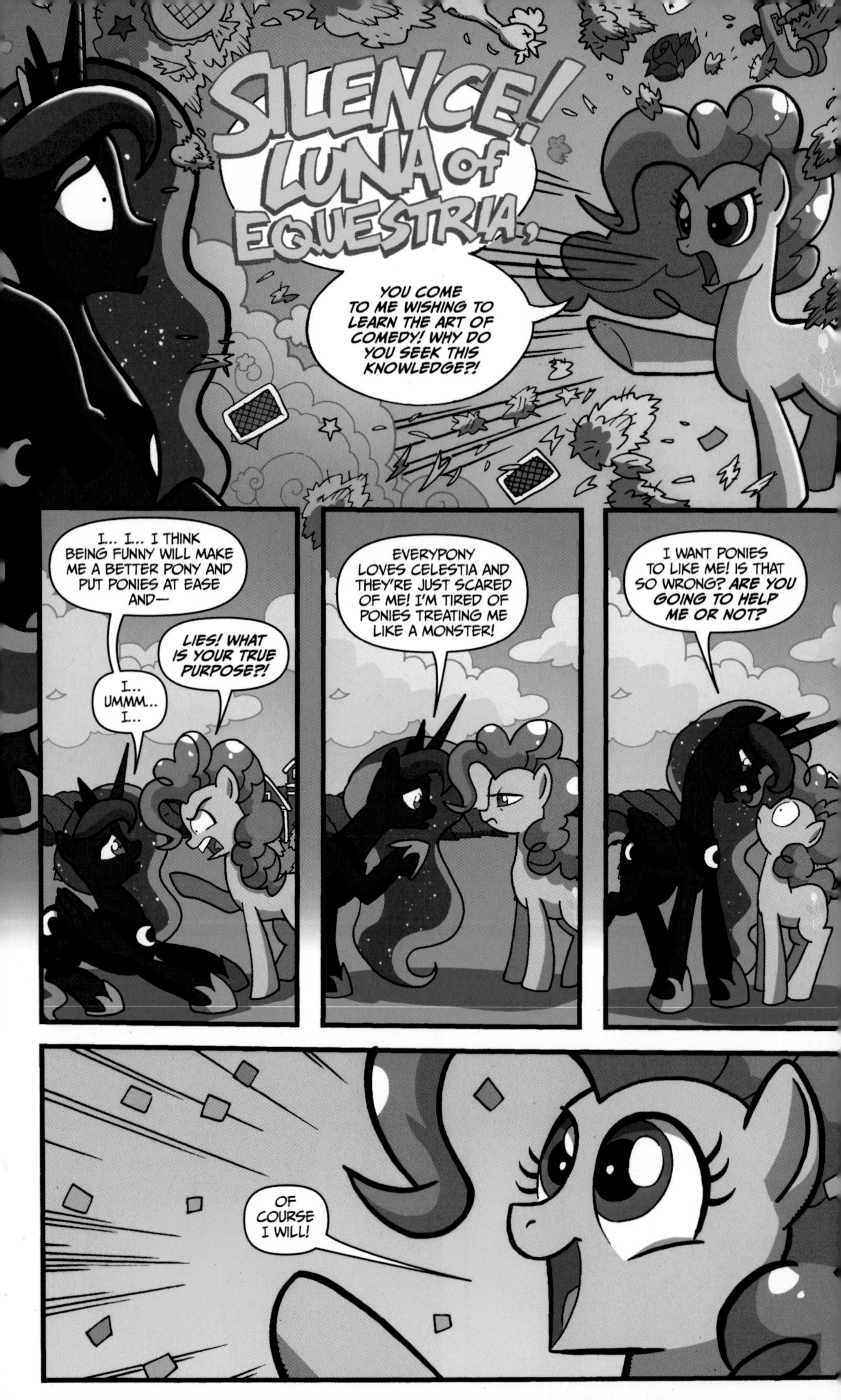
SILENCE! LUNA of EQUESTRIA,
YOU COME TO ME WISHING TO LEARN THE ART OF COMEDY! WHY DO YOU SEEK THIS KNOWLEDGE?!
I... I... I THINK BEING FUNNY WILL MAKE ME A BETTER PONY AND PUT PONIES AT EASE AND—
LIES! WHAT IS YOUR TRUE PURPOSE?!
I... UMMM... I...
EVERYPONY LOVES CELESTIA AND THEY'RE JUST SCARED OF ME! I'M TIRED OF PONIES TREATING ME LIKE A MONSTER!
I WANT PONIES TO LIKE ME! IS THAT SO WRONG? ARE YOU GOING TO HELP ME OR NOT?
OF COURSE I WILL!

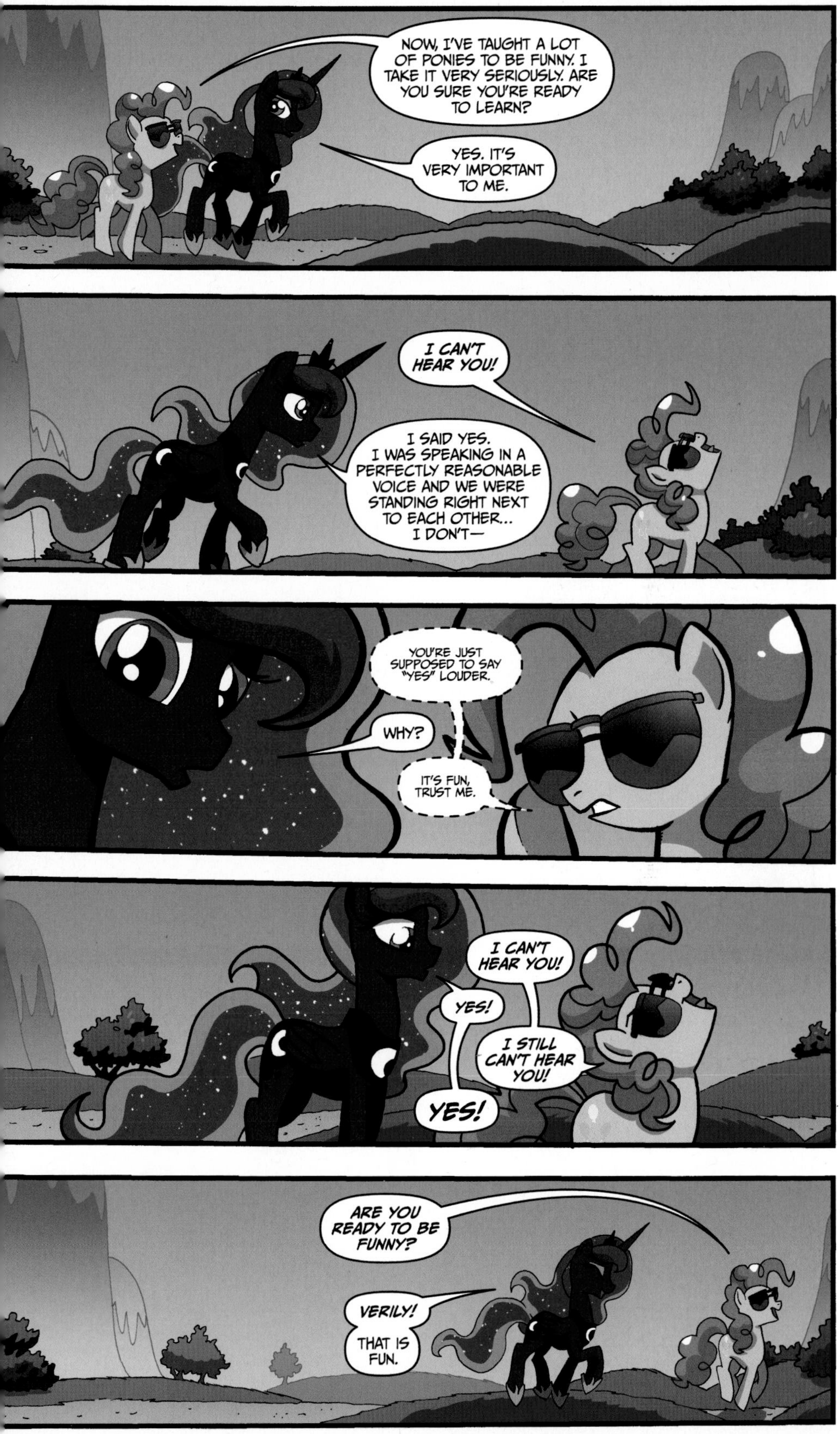
NOW, I'VE TAUGHT A LOT OF PONIES TO BE FUNNY. I TAKE IT VERY SERIOUSLY. ARE YOU SURE YOU'RE READY TO LEARN?
YES. IT'S VERY IMPORTANT TO ME.
I CAN'T HEAR YOU!
I SAID YES. I WAS SPEAKING IN A PERFECTLY REASONABLE VOICE AND WE WERE STANDING RIGHT NEXT TO EACH OTHER... I DON'T—
YOU'RE JUST SUPPOSED TO SAY "YES" LOUDER.
WHY?
IT'S FUN, TRUST ME.
I CAN'T HEAR YOU!
YES!
I STILL CAN'T HEAR YOU!
YES!
ARE YOU READY TO BE FUNNY?
VERILY!
THAT IS FUN.

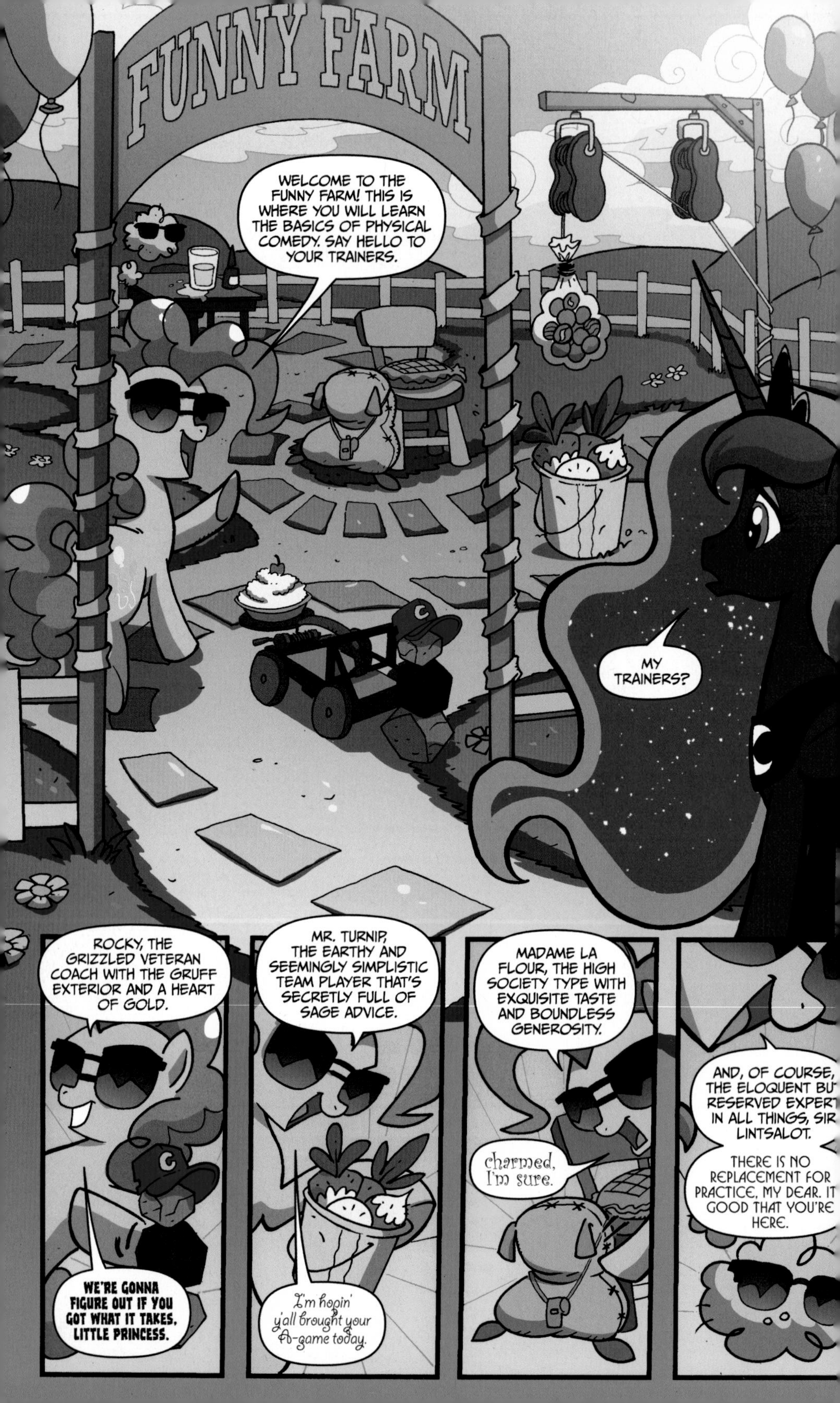

FUNNY FARM
WELCOME TO THE FUNNY FARM! THIS IS WHERE YOU WILL LEARN THE BASICS OF PHYSICAL COMEDY. SAY HELLO TO YOUR TRAINERS.
MY TRAINERS?
ROCKY, THE GRIZZLED VETERAN COACH WITH THE GRUFF EXTERIOR AND A HEART OF GOLD.
WE'RE GONNA FIGURE OUT IF YOU GOT WHAT IT TAKES, LITTLE PRINCESS.
MR. TURNIP, THE EARTHY AND SEEMINGLY SIMPLISTIC TEAM PLAYER THAT'S SECRETLY FULL OF SAGE ADVICE.
I'm hopin' y'all brought your A-game today.
MADAME LA FLOUR, THE HIGH SOCIETY TYPE WITH EXQUISITE TASTE AND BOUNDLESS GENEROSITY.
charmed, I'm sure.
AND, OF COURSE, THE ELOQUENT BU RESERVED EXPER IN ALL THINGS, SIR LINTSALOT.
THERE IS NO REPLACEMENT FOR PRACTICE, MY DEAR. IT GOOD THAT YOU'RE HERE.

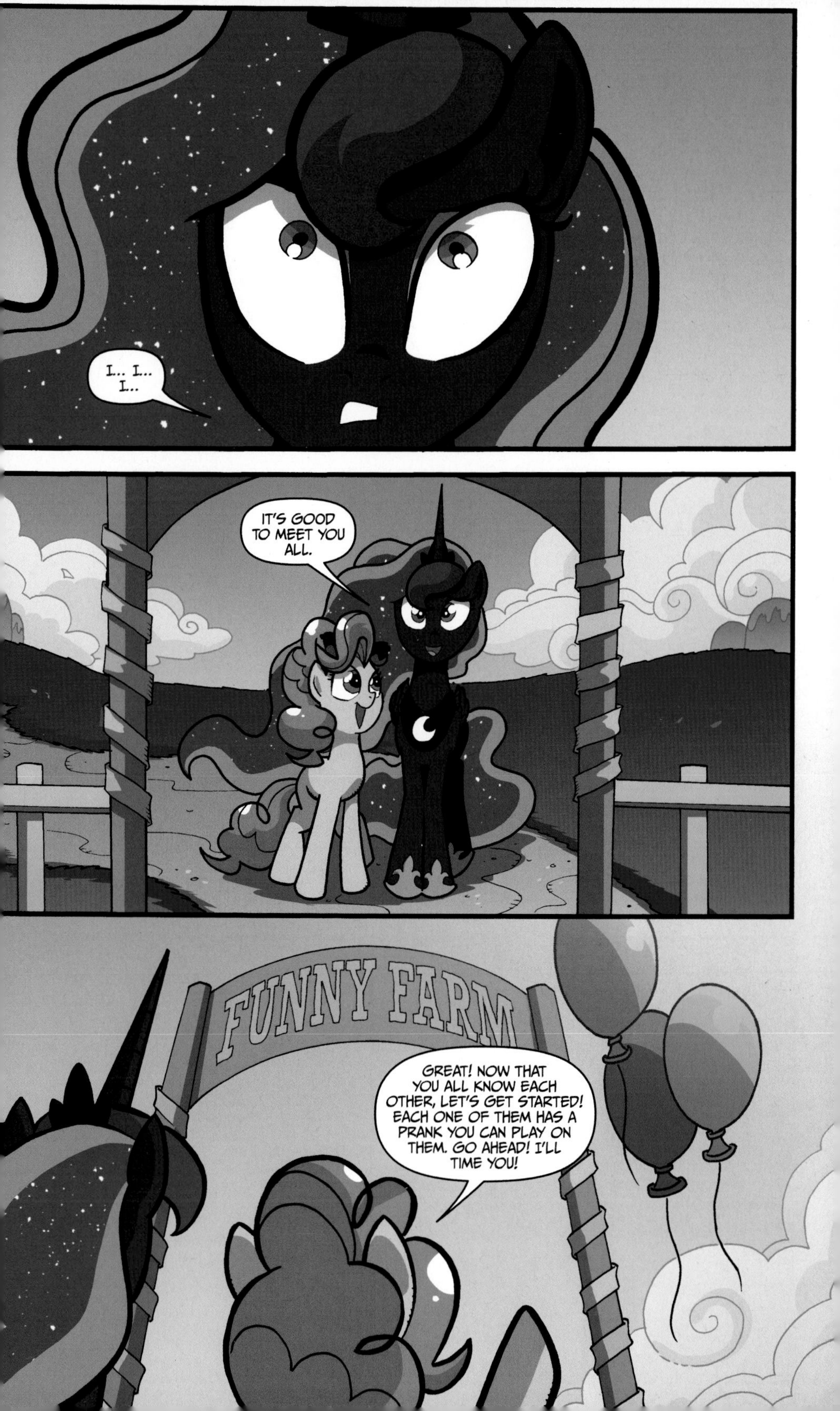
I... I... I...
IT'S GOOD TO MEET YOU ALL.
FUNNY FARM
GREAT! NOW THAT YOU ALL KNOW EACH OTHER, LET'S GET STARTED! EACH ONE OF THEM HAS A PRANK YOU CAN PLAY ON THEM. GO AHEAD! I'LL TIME YOU!

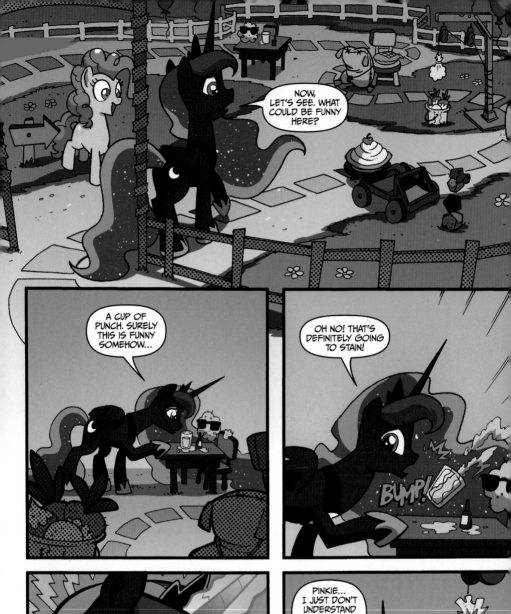

NOW, LET'S SEE. WHAT COULD BE FUNNY HERE?

A CUP OF PUNCH. SURELY THIS IS FUNNY SOMEHOW...

OH NO! THAT'S DEFINITELY GOING TO STAIN!

BUMP!

CATCH

SUPER GLUE

PINKIE... I JUST DON'T UNDERSTAND WHAT I'M SUPPOSED TO DO HERE.

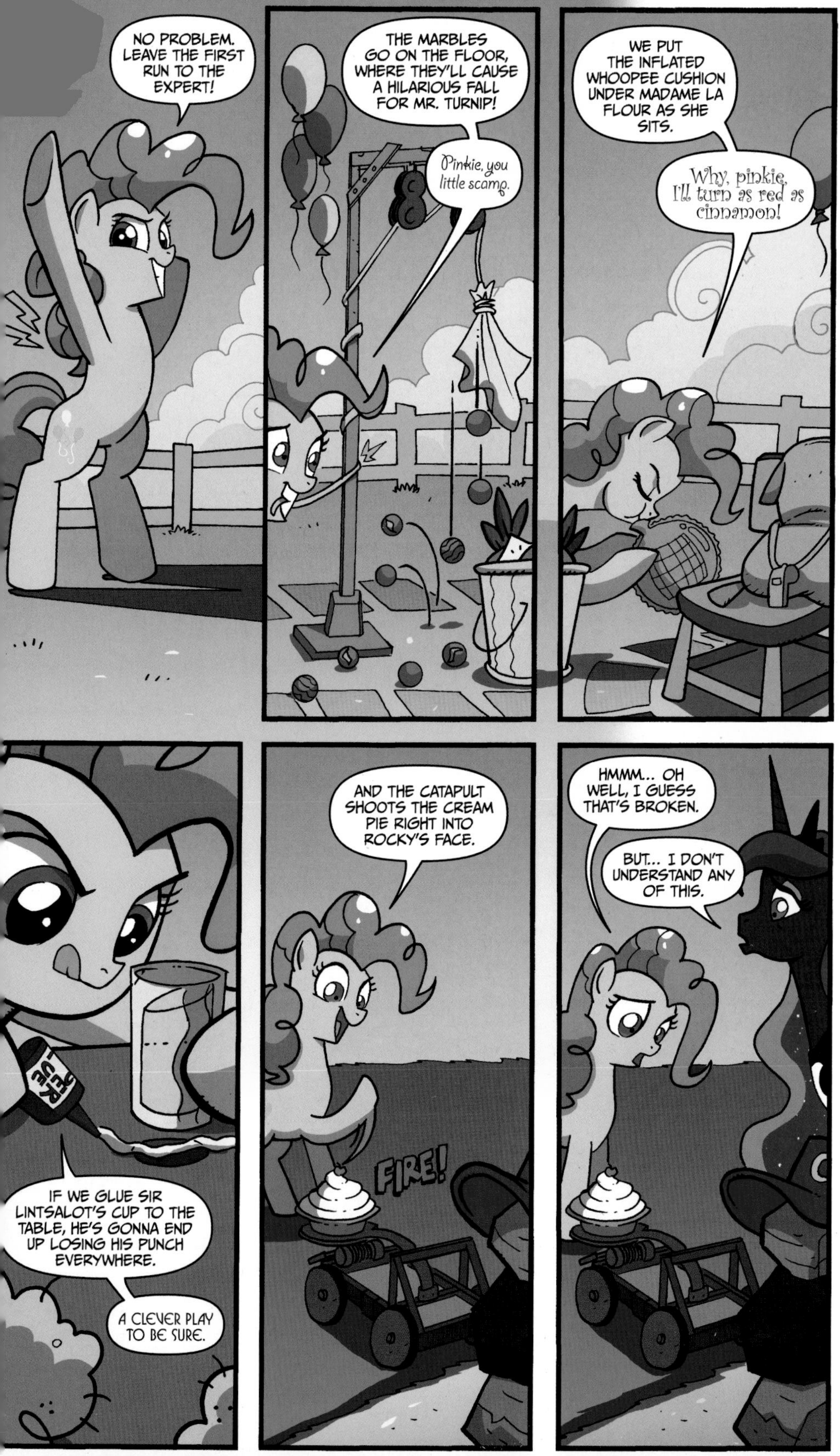
NO PROBLEM. LEAVE THE FIRST RUN TO THE EXPERT!
THE MARBLES GO ON THE FLOOR, WHERE THEY'LL CAUSE A HILARIOUS FALL FOR MR. TURNIP!
Pinkie, you little scamp.
WE PUT THE INFLATED WHOOPEE CUSHION UNDER MADAME LA FLOUR AS SHE SITS.
Why, pinkie, I'll turn as red as cinnamon!
IF WE GLUE SIR LINTSALOT'S CUP TO THE TABLE, HE'S GONNA END UP LOSING HIS PUNCH EVERYWHERE.
A CLEVER PLAY TO BE SURE.
AND THE CATAPULT SHOOTS THE CREAM PIE RIGHT INTO ROCKY'S FACE.
FIRE!
HMMM... OH WELL, I GUESS THAT'S BROKEN.
BUT... I DON'T UNDERSTAND ANY OF THIS.

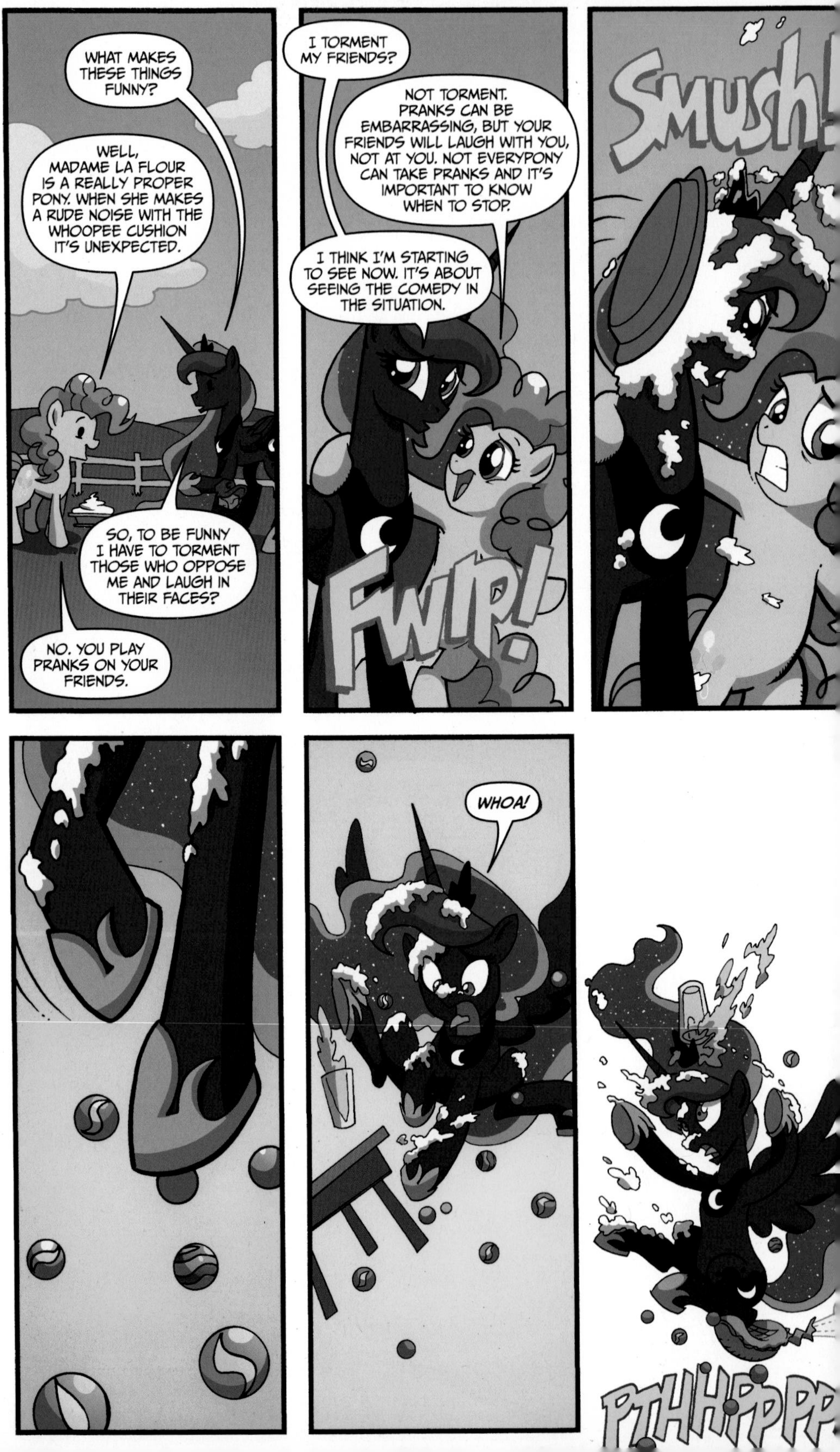
WHAT MAKES THESE THINGS FUNNY?
WELL, MADAME LA FLOUR IS A REALLY PROPER PONY. WHEN SHE MAKES A RUDE NOISE WITH THE WHOOPEE CUSHION IT'S UNEXPECTED.
SO, TO BE FUNNY I HAVE TO TORMENT THOSE WHO OPPOSE ME AND LAUGH IN THEIR FACES?
NO. YOU PLAY PRANKS ON YOUR FRIENDS.
I TORMENT MY FRIENDS?
NOT TORMENT. PRANKS CAN BE EMBARRASSING, BUT YOUR FRIENDS WILL LAUGH WITH YOU, NOT AT YOU. NOT EVERYPONY CAN TAKE PRANKS AND IT'S IMPORTANT TO KNOW WHEN TO STOP.
I THINK I'M STARTING TO SEE NOW. IT'S ABOUT SEEING THE COMEDY IN THE SITUATION.
FWIP!
SMUSH!
WHOA!
PTHHPPPP

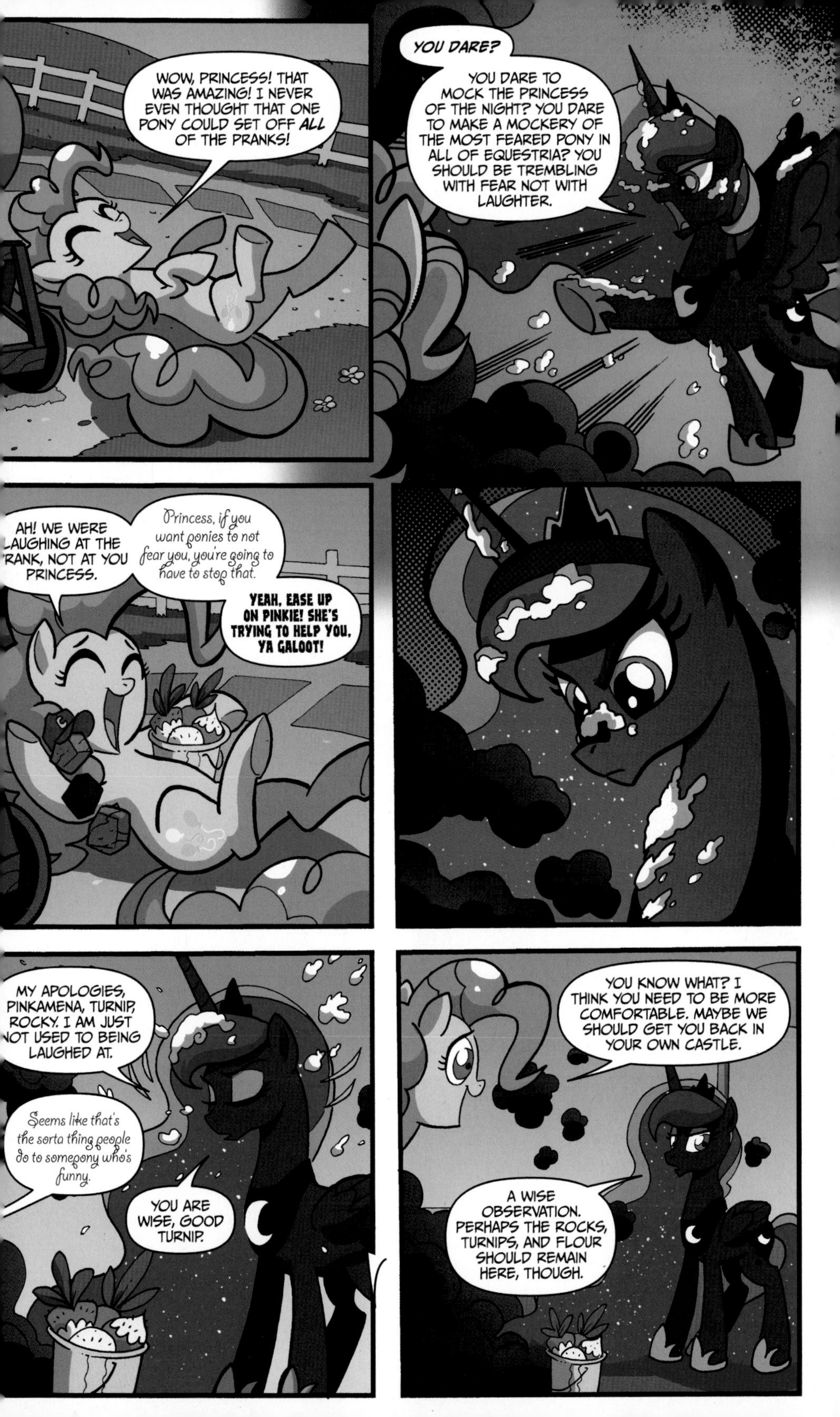
WOW, PRINCESS! THAT WAS AMAZING! I NEVER EVEN THOUGHT THAT ONE PONY COULD SET OFF ALL OF THE PRANKS!
YOU DARE?
YOU DARE TO MOCK THE PRINCESS OF THE NIGHT? YOU DARE TO MAKE A MOCKERY OF THE MOST FEARED PONY IN ALL OF EQUESTRIA? YOU SHOULD BE TREMBLING WITH FEAR NOT WITH LAUGHTER.
AH! WE WERE LAUGHING AT THE PRANK, NOT AT YOU PRINCESS.
Princess, if you want ponies to not fear you, you're going to have to stop that.
YEAH, EASE UP ON PINKIE! SHE'S TRYING TO HELP YOU, YA GALOOT!
MY APOLOGIES, PINKAMENA, TURNIP, ROCKY. I AM JUST NOT USED TO BEING LAUGHED AT.
Seems like that's the sorta thing people do to somepony who's funny.
YOU ARE WISE, GOOD TURNIP.
YOU KNOW WHAT? I THINK YOU NEED TO BE MORE COMFORTABLE. MAYBE WE SHOULD GET YOU BACK IN YOUR OWN CASTLE.
A WISE OBSERVATION. PERHAPS THE ROCKS, TURNIPS, AND FLOUR SHOULD REMAIN HERE, THOUGH.

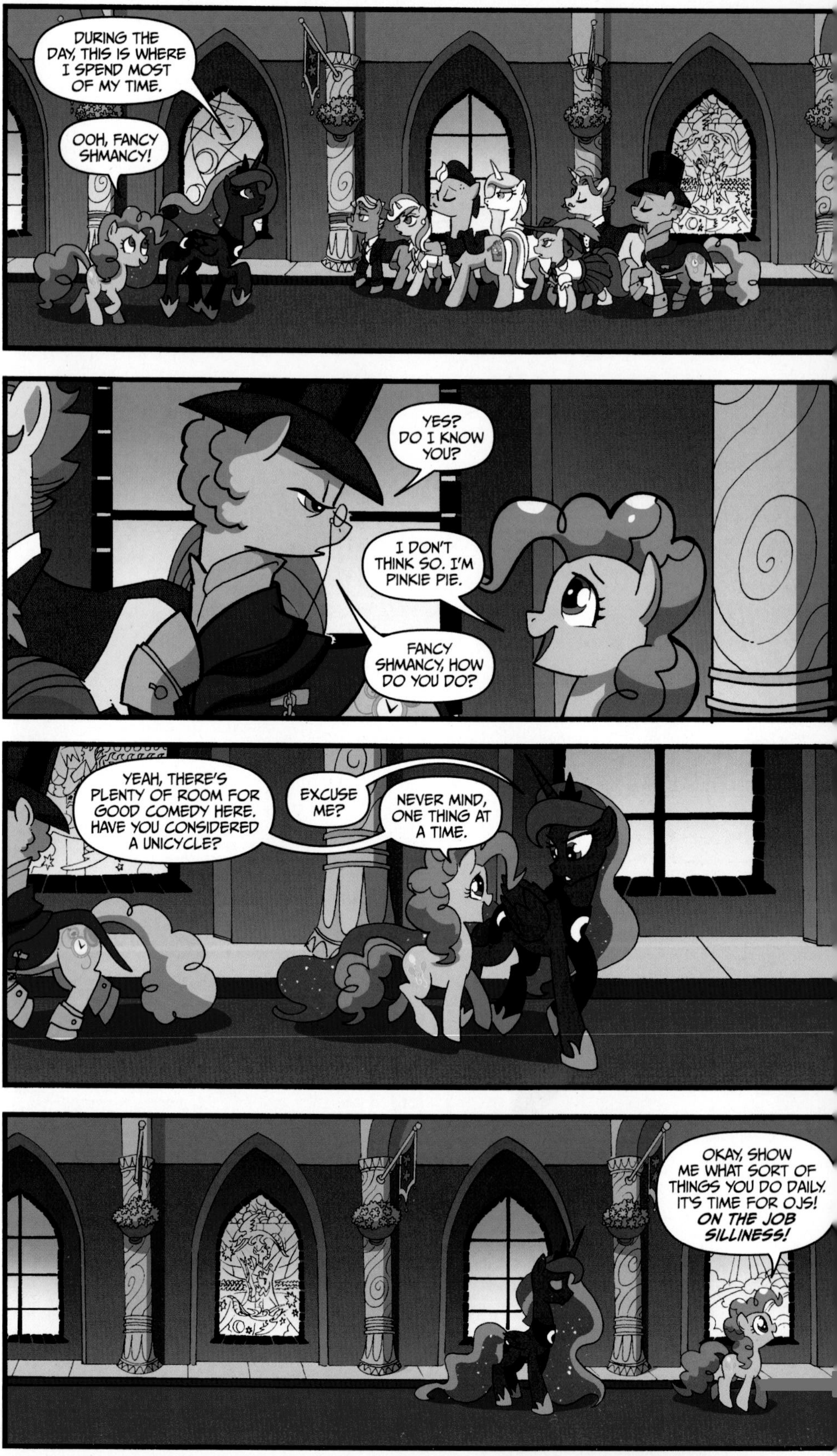
DURING THE DAY, THIS IS WHERE I SPEND MOST OF MY TIME.
OOH, FANCY SHMANCY!
YES? DO I KNOW YOU?
I DON'T THINK SO. I'M PINKIE PIE.
FANCY SHMANCY, HOW DO YOU DO?
YEAH, THERE'S PLENTY OF ROOM FOR GOOD COMEDY HERE. HAVE YOU CONSIDERED A UNICYCLE?
EXCUSE ME?
NEVER MIND, ONE THING AT A TIME.
OKAY, SHOW ME WHAT SORT OF THINGS YOU DO DAILY. IT'S TIME FOR OJS! ***ON THE JOB SILLINESS!***

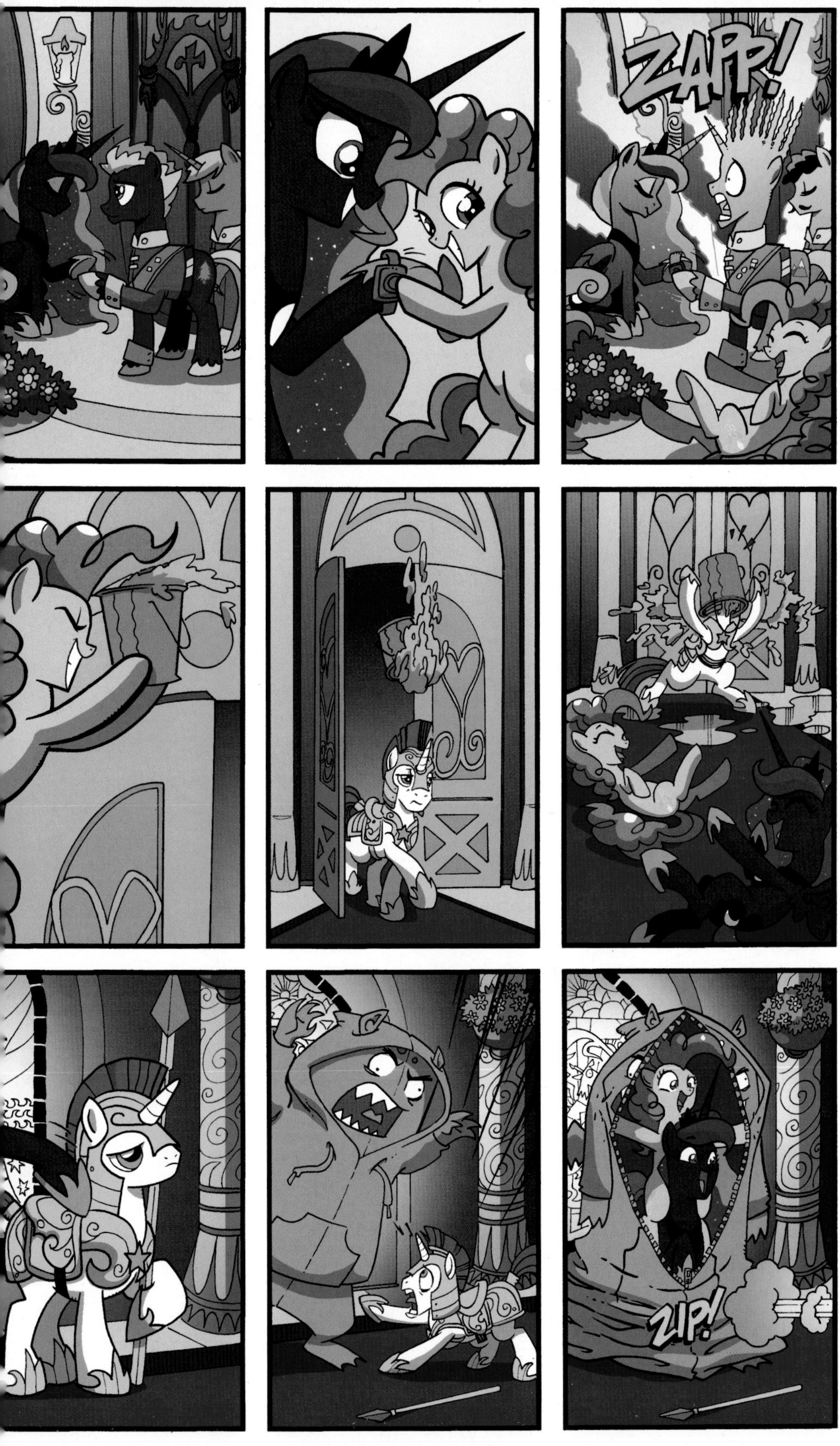
ZAPP!
ZIP!

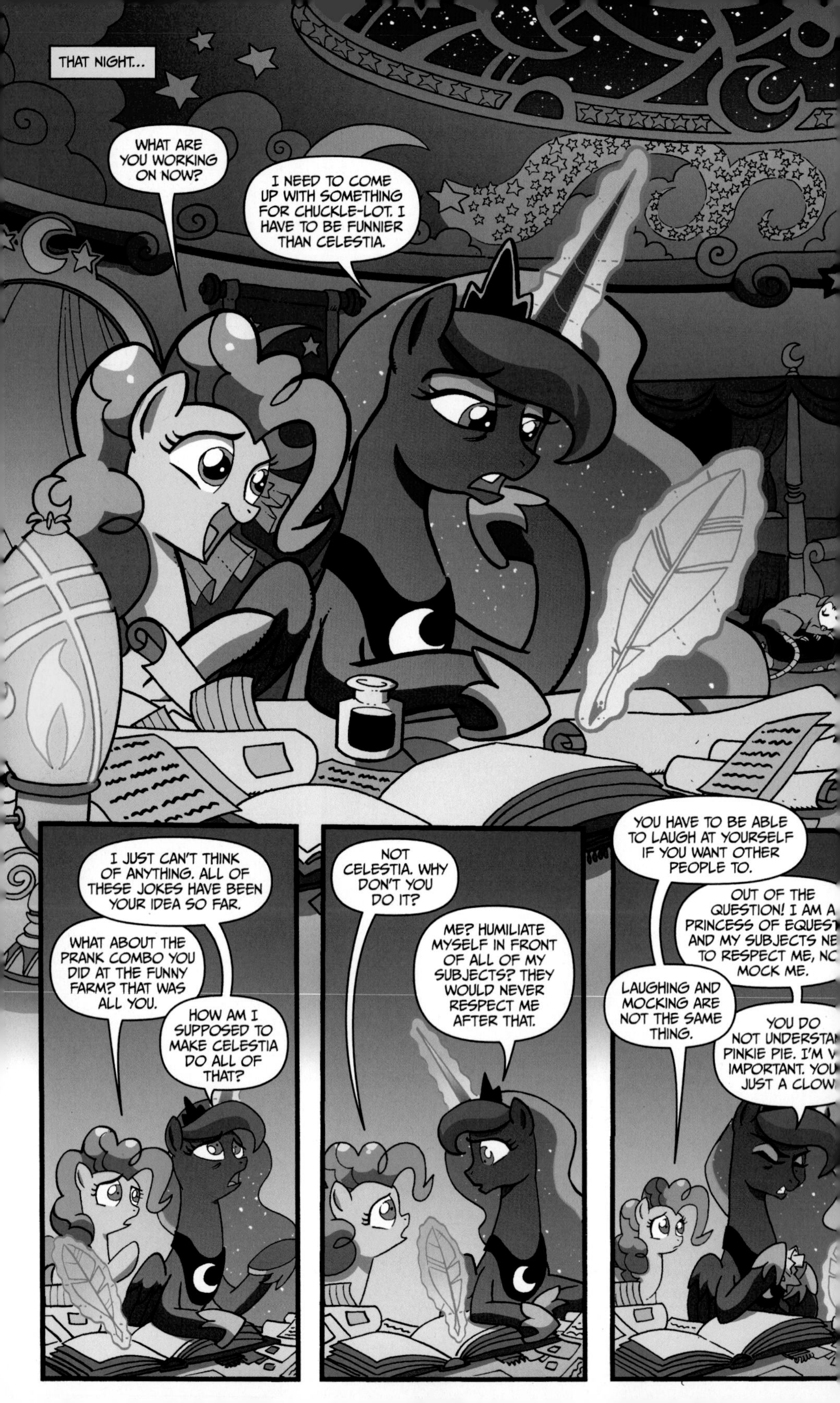
THAT NIGHT...
WHAT ARE YOU WORKING ON NOW?
I NEED TO COME UP WITH SOMETHING FOR CHUCKLE-LOT. I HAVE TO BE FUNNIER THAN CELESTIA.
I JUST CAN'T THINK OF ANYTHING. ALL OF THESE JOKES HAVE BEEN YOUR IDEA SO FAR.
WHAT ABOUT THE PRANK COMBO YOU DID AT THE FUNNY FARM? THAT WAS ALL YOU.
HOW AM I SUPPOSED TO MAKE CELESTIA DO ALL OF THAT?
NOT CELESTIA. WHY DON'T YOU DO IT?
ME? HUMILIATE MYSELF IN FRONT OF ALL OF MY SUBJECTS? THEY WOULD NEVER RESPECT ME AFTER THAT.
YOU HAVE TO BE ABLE TO LAUGH AT YOURSELF IF YOU WANT OTHER PEOPLE TO.
OUT OF THE QUESTION! I AM A PRINCESS OF EQUEST AND MY SUBJECTS NE TO RESPECT ME, NO MOCK ME.
LAUGHING AND MOCKING ARE NOT THE SAME THING.
YOU DO NOT UNDERSTAN PINKIE PIE. I'M V IMPORTANT. YOU JUST A CLOW

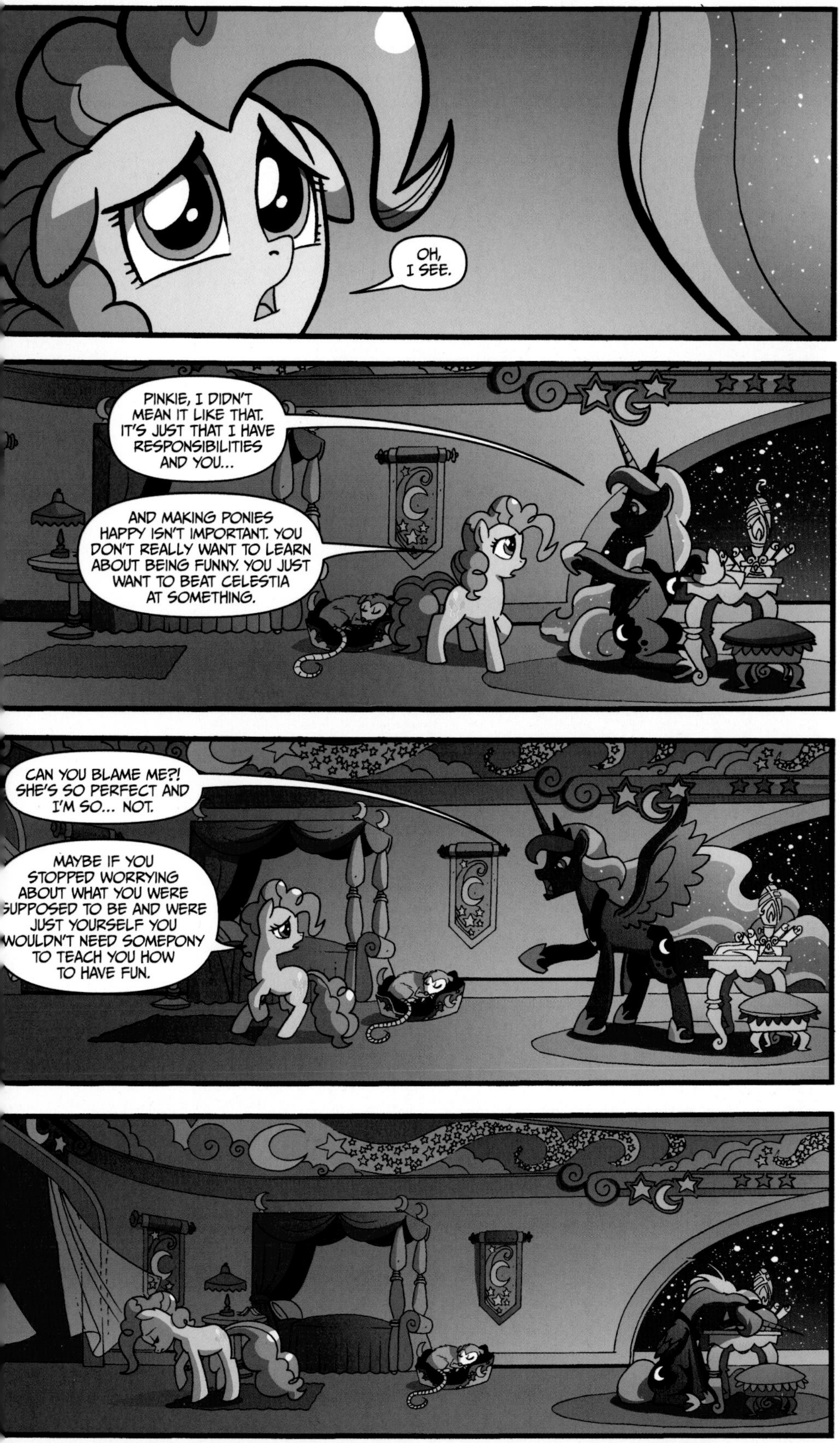
OH, I SEE.
PINKIE, I DIDN'T MEAN IT LIKE THAT. IT'S JUST THAT I HAVE RESPONSIBILITIES AND YOU...
AND MAKING PONIES HAPPY ISN'T IMPORTANT. YOU DON'T REALLY WANT TO LEARN ABOUT BEING FUNNY. YOU JUST WANT TO BEAT CELESTIA AT SOMETHING.
CAN YOU BLAME ME?! SHE'S SO PERFECT AND I'M SO... NOT.
MAYBE IF YOU STOPPED WORRYING ABOUT WHAT YOU WERE SUPPOSED TO BE AND WERE JUST YOURSELF YOU WOULDN'T NEED SOMEPONY TO TEACH YOU HOW TO HAVE FUN.

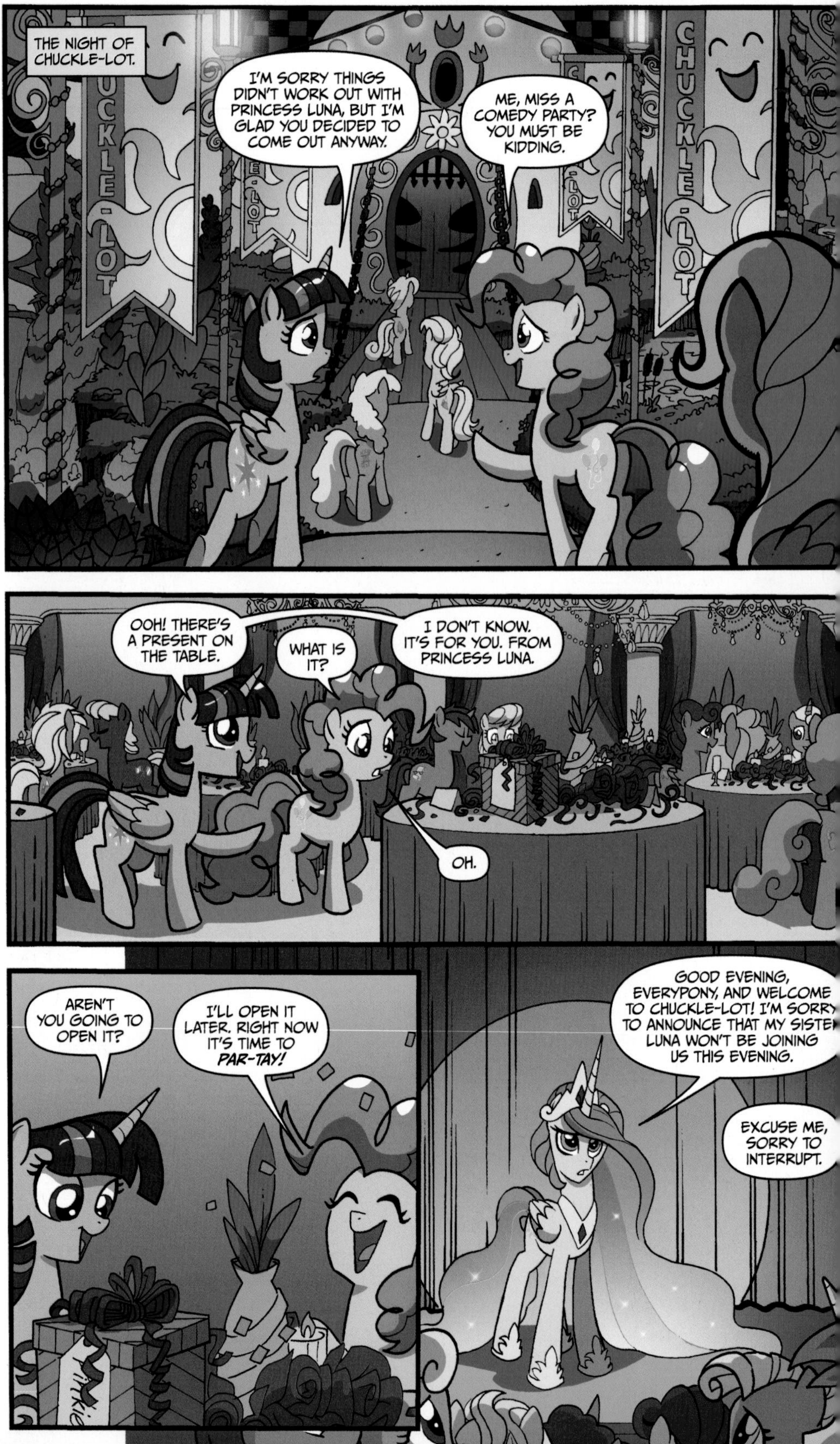
THE NIGHT OF CHUCKLE-LOT.
CHUCKLE-LOT
I'M SORRY THINGS DIDN'T WORK OUT WITH PRINCESS LUNA, BUT I'M GLAD YOU DECIDED TO COME OUT ANYWAY.
ME, MISS A COMEDY PARTY? YOU MUST BE KIDDING.
CHUCKLE-LOT
OOH! THERE'S A PRESENT ON THE TABLE.
WHAT IS IT?
I DON'T KNOW. IT'S FOR YOU. FROM PRINCESS LUNA.
OH.
AREN'T YOU GOING TO OPEN IT?
I'LL OPEN IT LATER. RIGHT NOW IT'S TIME TO *PAR-TAY!*
GOOD EVENING, EVERYPONY, AND WELCOME TO CHUCKLE-LOT! I'M SORRY TO ANNOUNCE THAT MY SISTE LUNA WON'T BE JOINING US THIS EVENING.
EXCUSE ME, SORRY TO INTERRUPT.

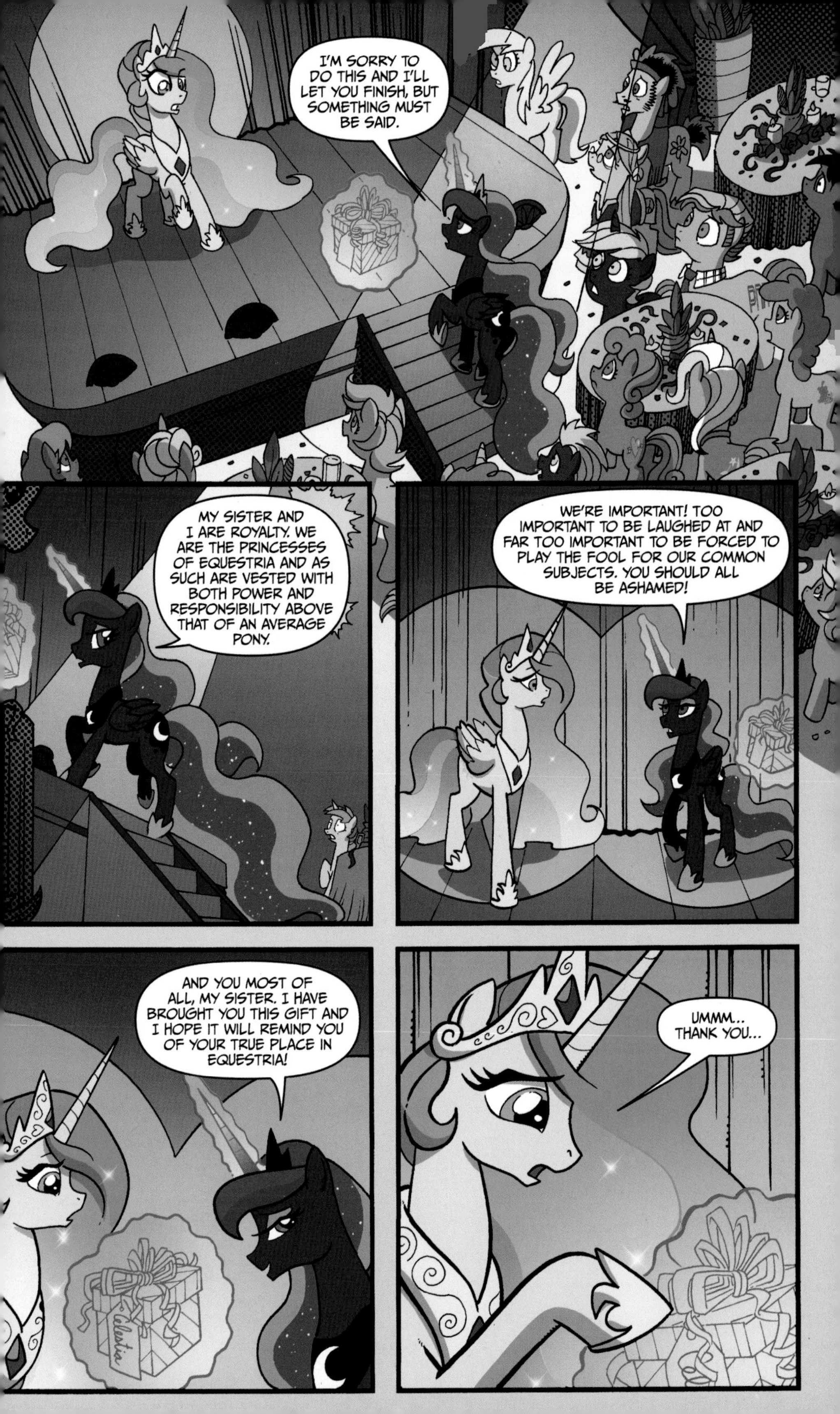
I'M SORRY TO DO THIS AND I'LL LET YOU FINISH, BUT SOMETHING MUST BE SAID.
MY SISTER AND I ARE ROYALTY. WE ARE THE PRINCESSES OF EQUESTRIA AND AS SUCH ARE VESTED WITH BOTH POWER AND RESPONSIBILITY ABOVE THAT OF AN AVERAGE PONY.
WE'RE IMPORTANT! TOO IMPORTANT TO BE LAUGHED AT AND FAR TOO IMPORTANT TO BE FORCED TO PLAY THE FOOL FOR OUR COMMON SUBJECTS. YOU SHOULD ALL BE ASHAMED!
AND YOU MOST OF ALL, MY SISTER. I HAVE BROUGHT YOU THIS GIFT AND I HOPE IT WILL REMIND YOU OF YOUR TRUE PLACE IN EQUESTRIA!
UMMM... THANK YOU...

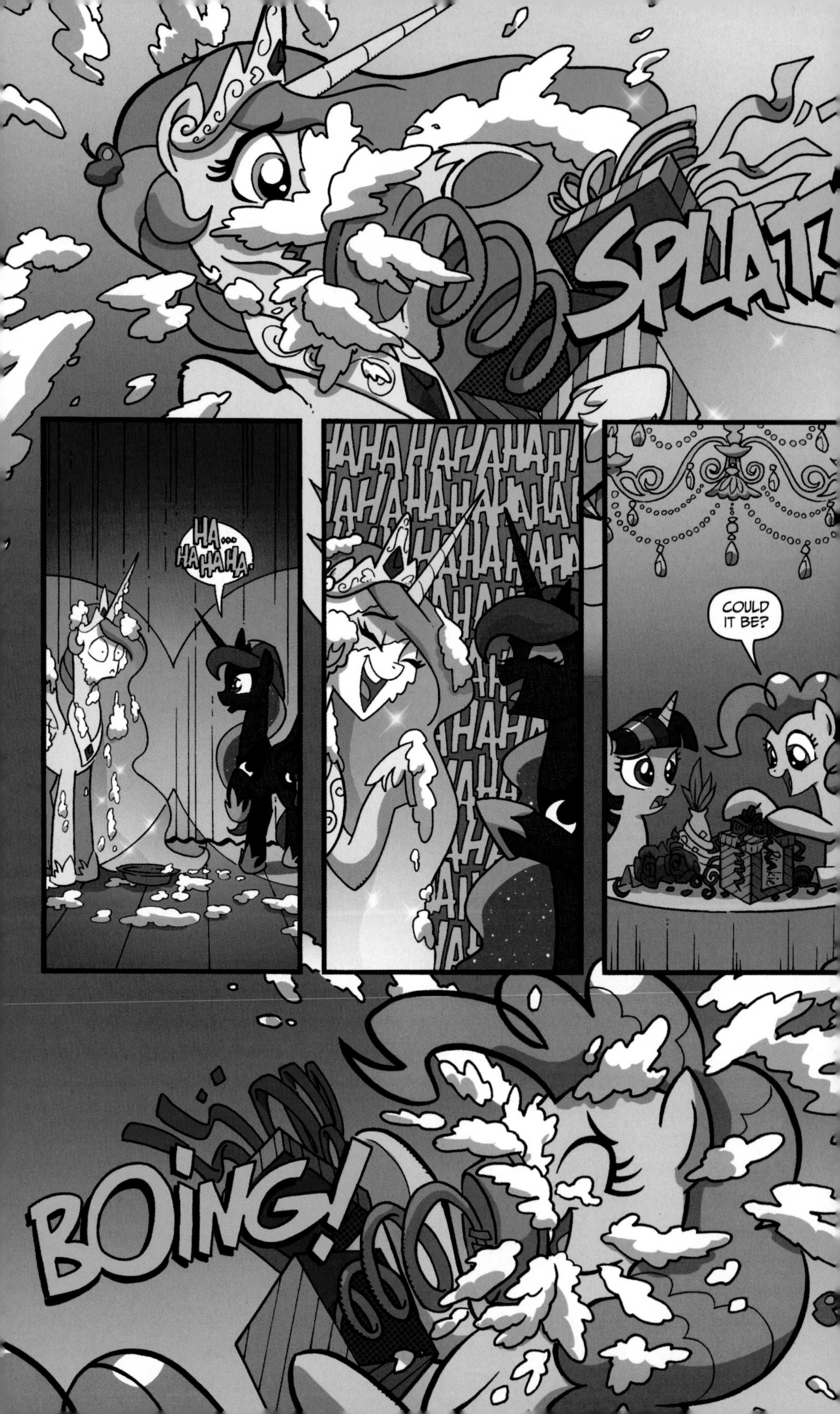
SPLAT!
HA... HA HA HA.
HAHA HAHAHAH!
COULD IT BE?
BOING!

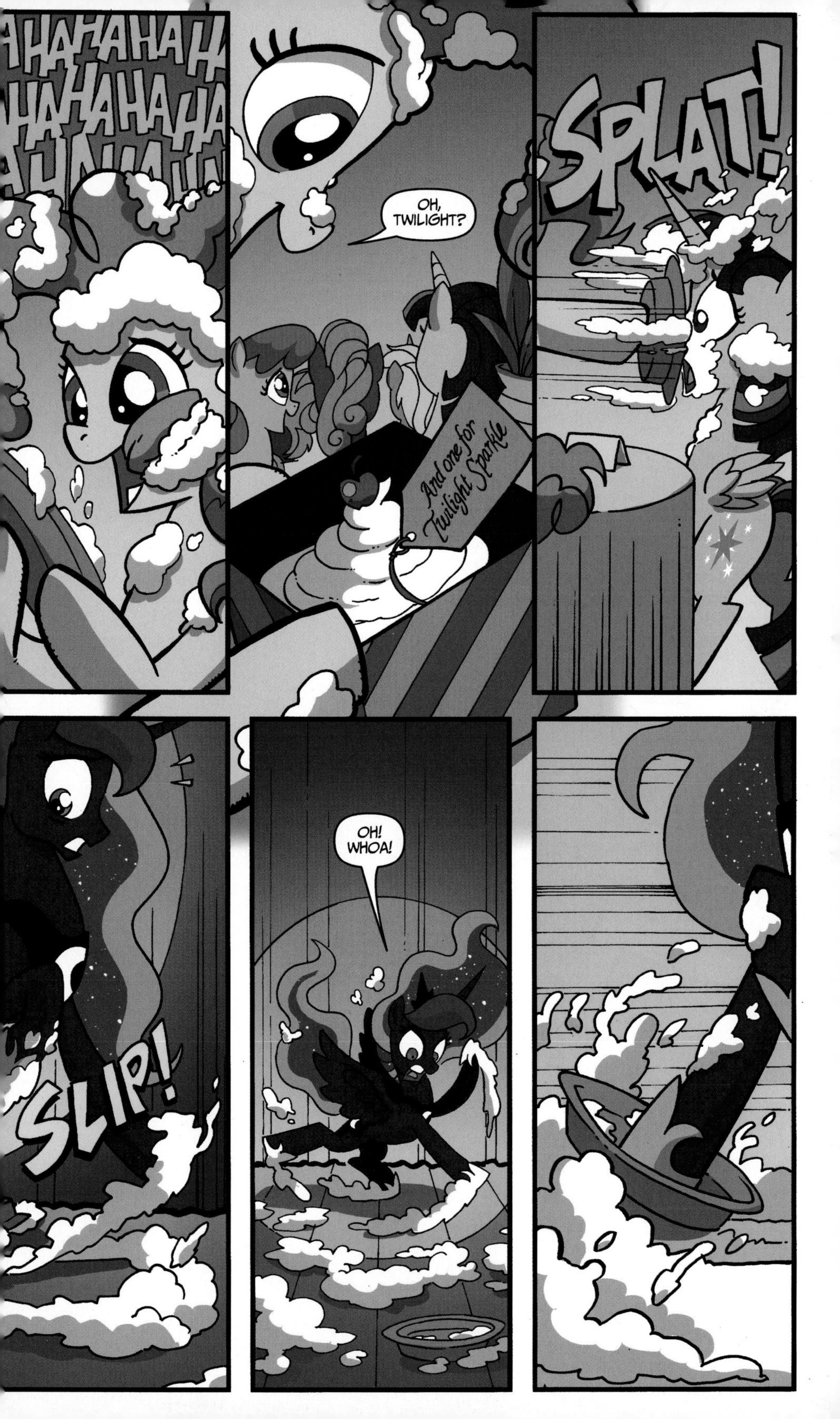
HAHAHAHAHAHAHAHAHA
OH, TWILIGHT?
And one for Twilight Sparkle
SPLAT!
SLIP!
OH! WHOA!

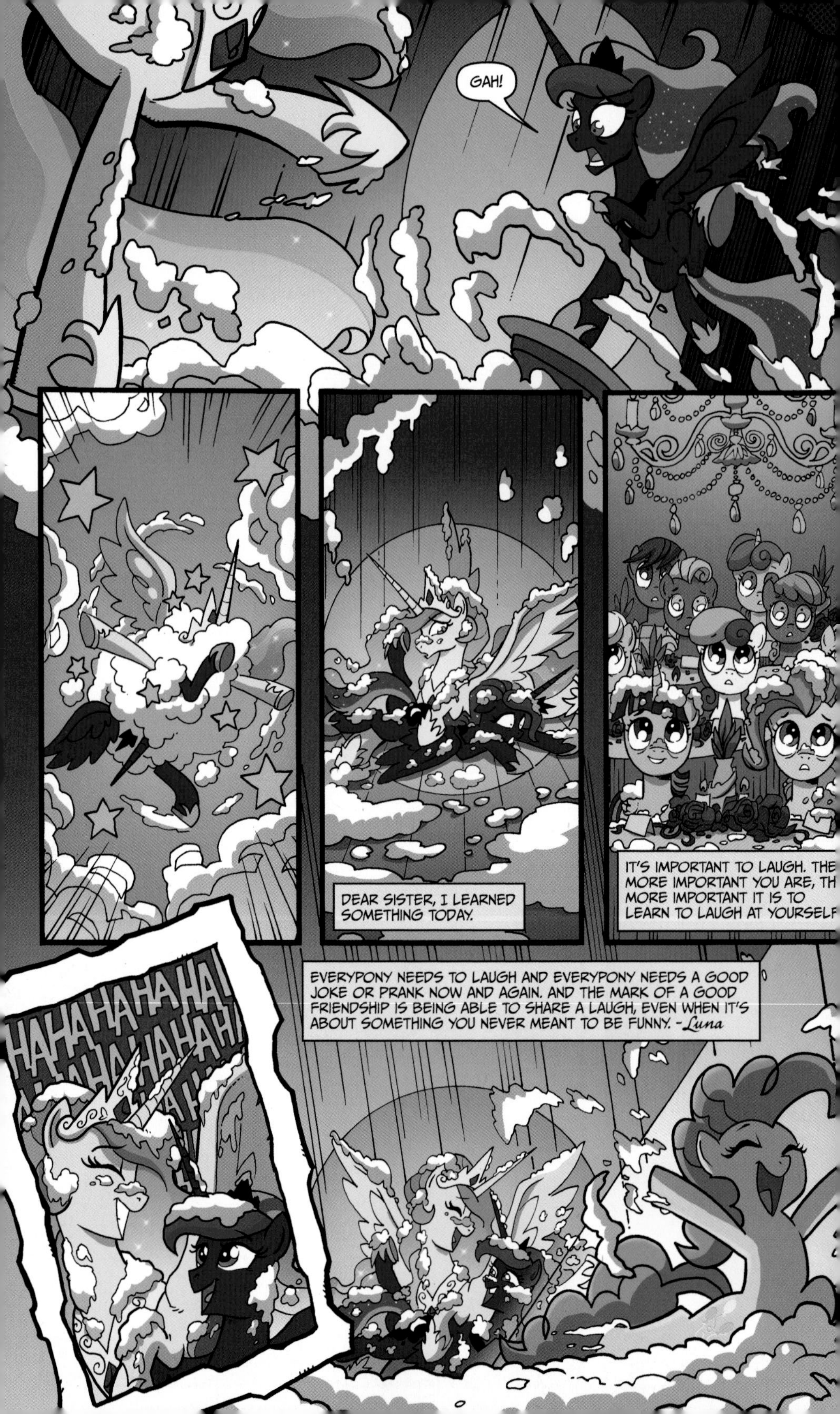
GAH!
DEAR SISTER, I LEARNED SOMETHING TODAY.
IT'S IMPORTANT TO LAUGH. THE MORE IMPORTANT YOU ARE, TH MORE IMPORTANT IT IS TO LEARN TO LAUGH AT YOURSELF
EVERYPONY NEEDS TO LAUGH AND EVERYPONY NEEDS A GOOD JOKE OR PRANK NOW AND AGAIN. AND THE MARK OF A GOOD FRIENDSHIP IS BEING ABLE TO SHARE A LAUGH, EVEN WHEN IT'S ABOUT SOMETHING YOU NEVER MEANT TO BE FUNNY. -Luna
HAHAHAHAHA! HAHAHAHAH!

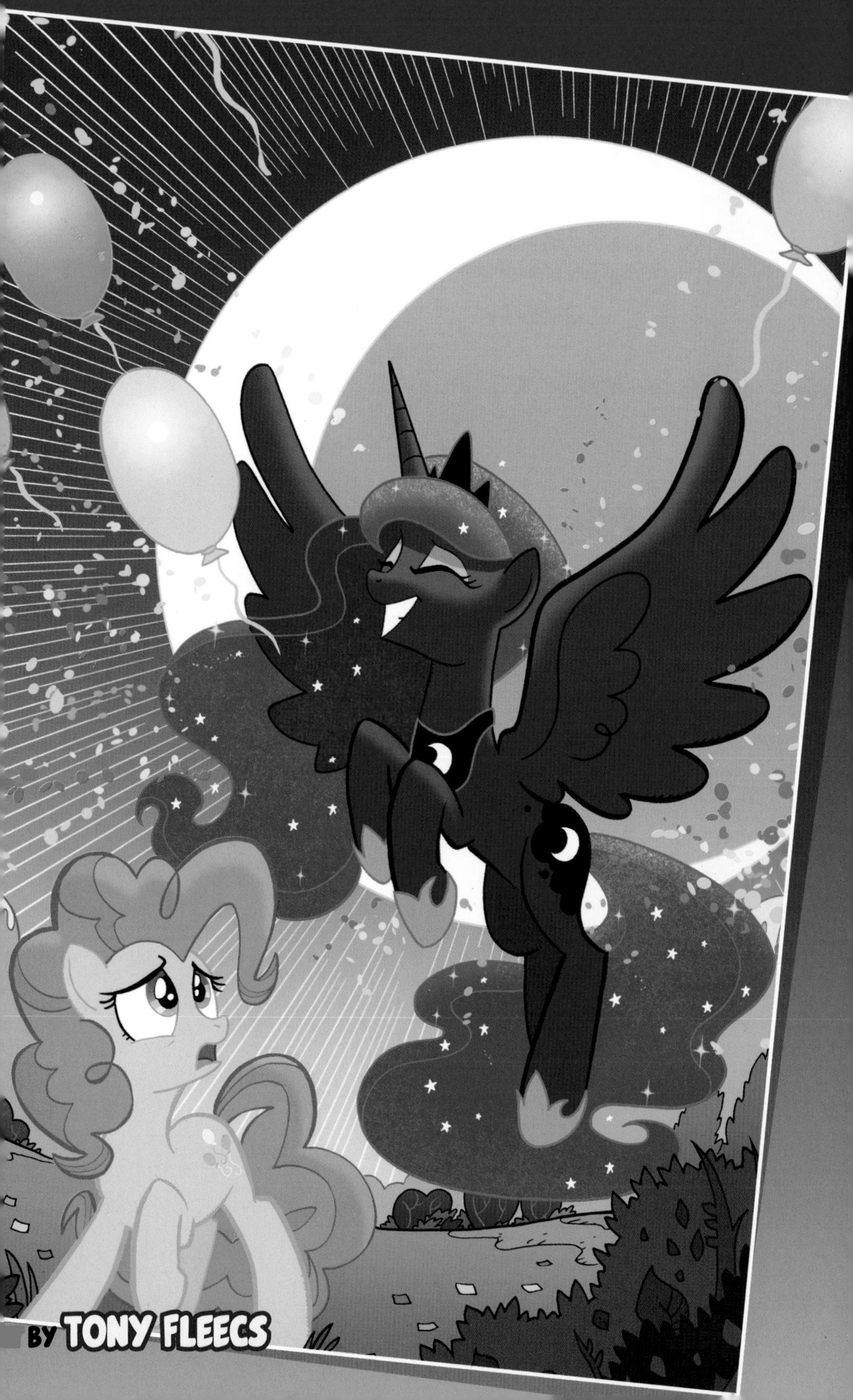
BY TONY FLEECS

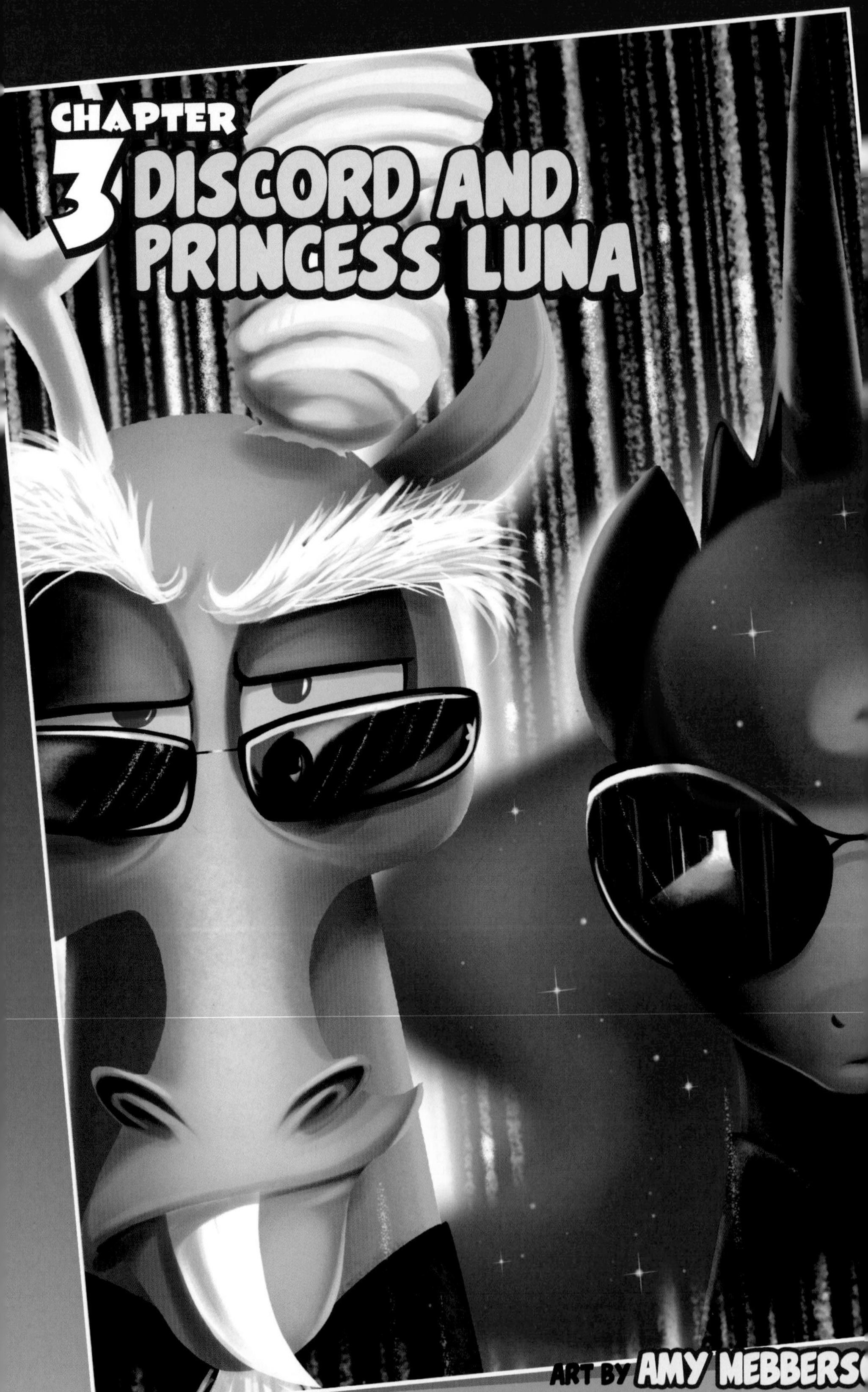
CHAPTER
3
DISCORD AND
PRINCESS LUNA
ART BY AMY MEBBERSO

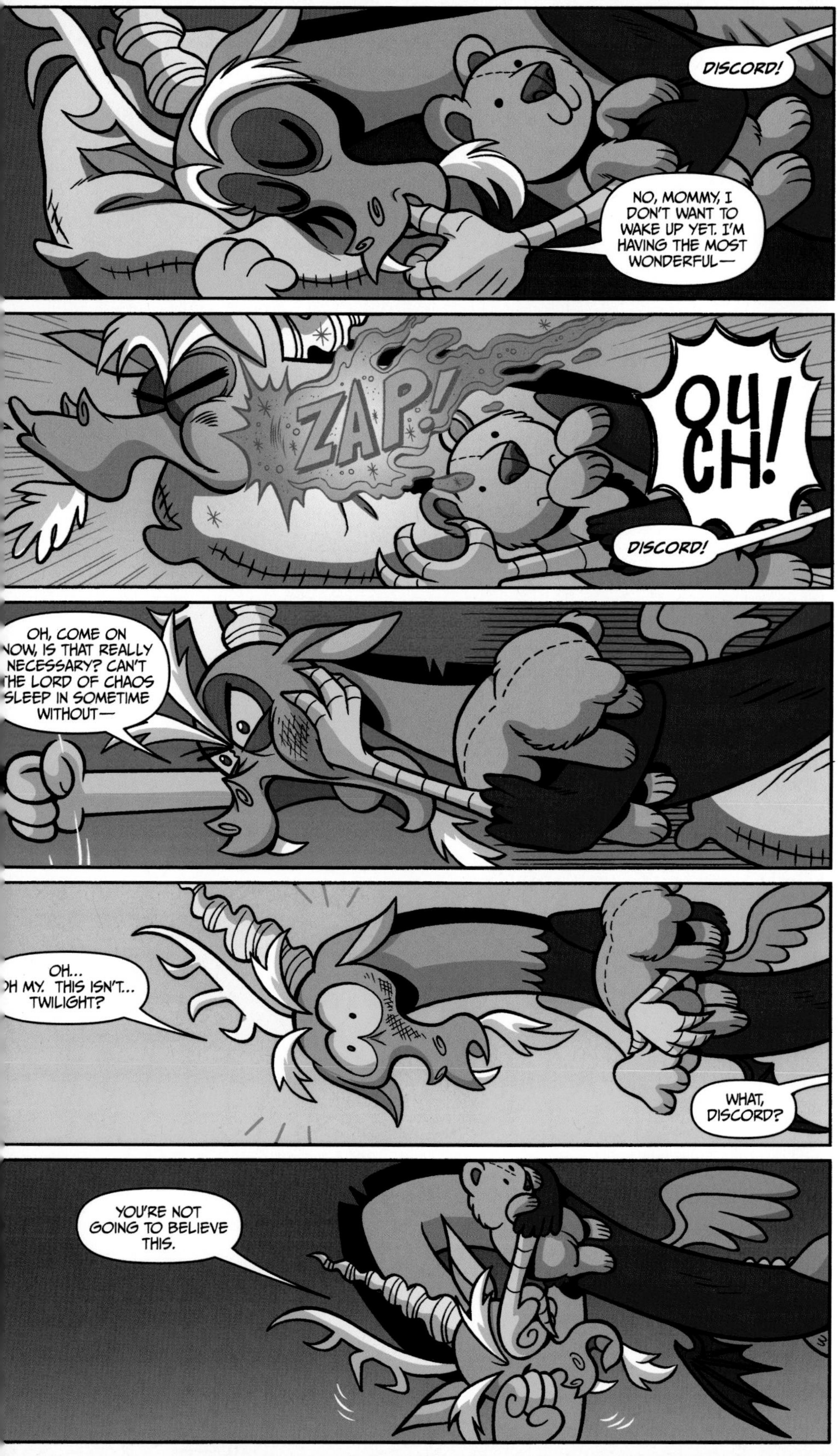
DISCORD!
NO, MOMMY, I DON'T WANT TO WAKE UP YET. I'M HAVING THE MOST WONDERFUL—
ZAP!
OUCH!
DISCORD!
OH, COME ON NOW, IS THAT REALLY NECESSARY? CAN'T THE LORD OF CHAOS SLEEP IN SOMETIME WITHOUT—
OH... OH MY. THIS ISN'T... TWILIGHT?
WHAT, DISCORD?
YOU'RE NOT GOING TO BELIEVE THIS.

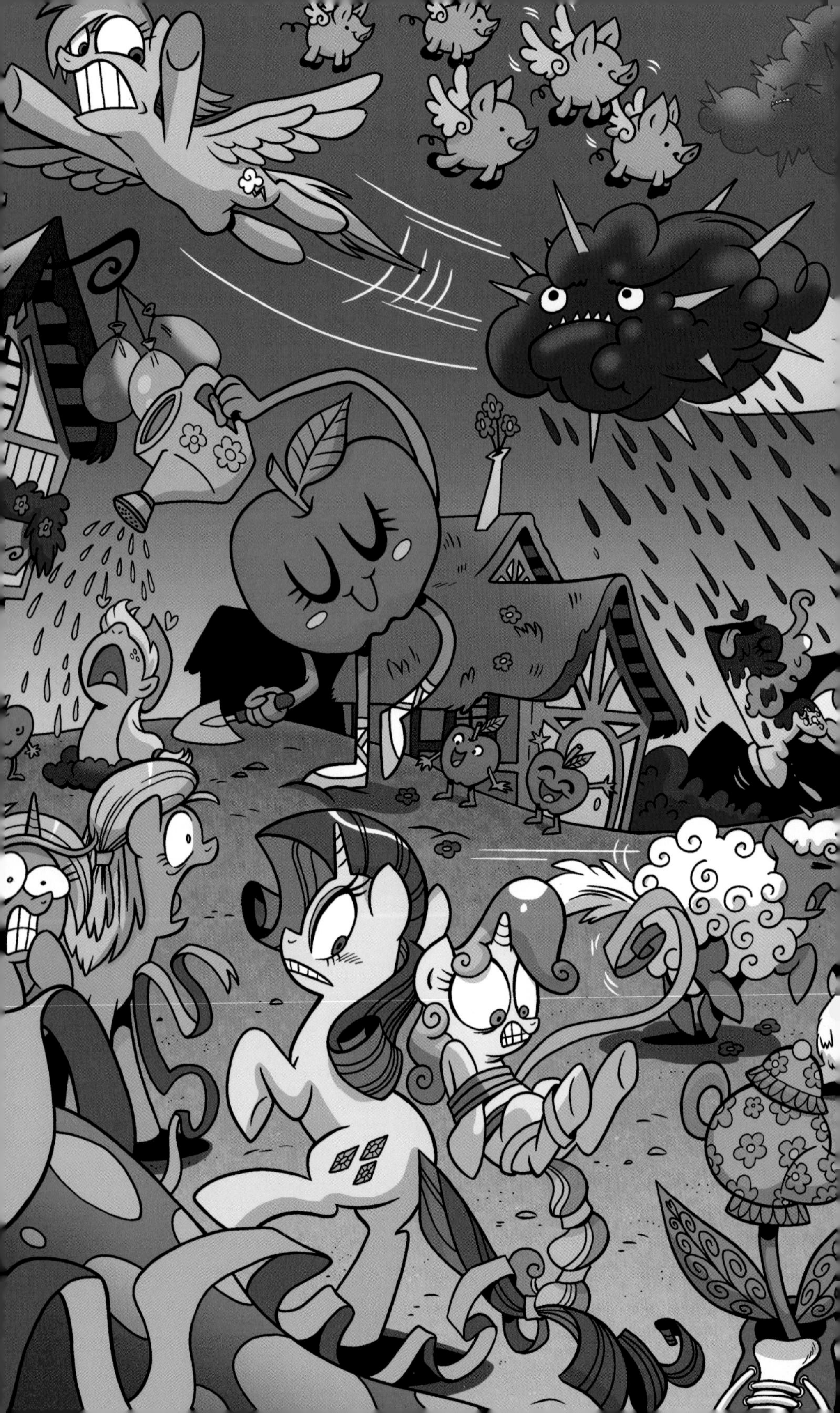

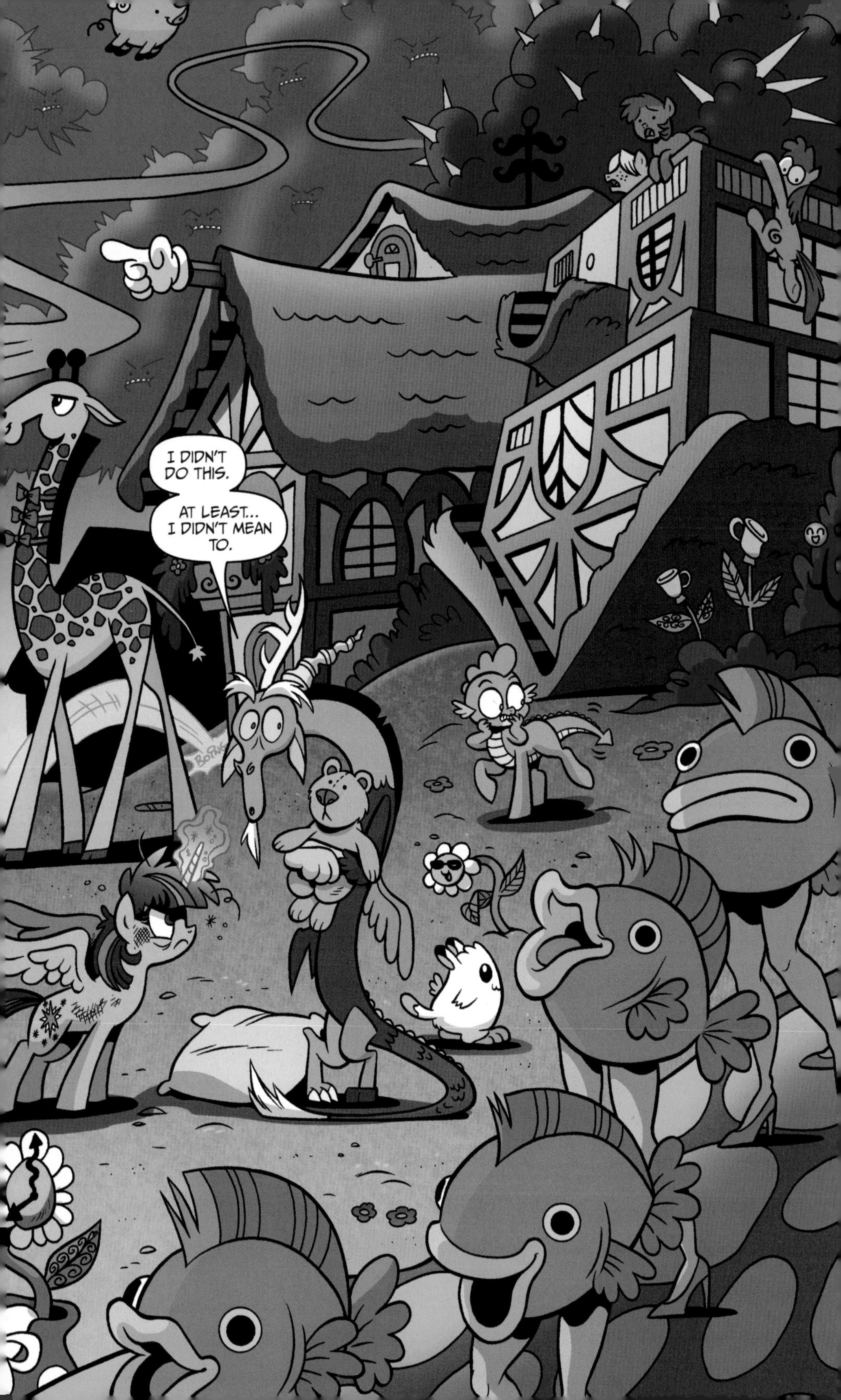
I DIDN'T DO THIS.
AT LEAST... I DIDN'T MEAN TO.
BOING

SLEEP WALKING?

THAT'S WHAT HE SAYS, YOUR MAJESTY. HE CLAIMS HE DESTROYED THE ENTIRE TOWN WITHOUT EVEN KNOWING IT.

I THINK I BELIEVE HIM. AS SOON AS I FINALLY MADE IT THROUGH THE MESS AND I ZAPPED HIM, HE OPENED HIS EYES AND EVERYTHING STOPPED.

BUT... SLEEPWALKING IS USUALLY A SIGN OF NIGHTMARES. SOMETHING UNDERLYING THAT'S BOTHERING A PONY. SOMETHING A PONY IS AFRAID OF. WHAT IS DISCORD AFRAID OF?

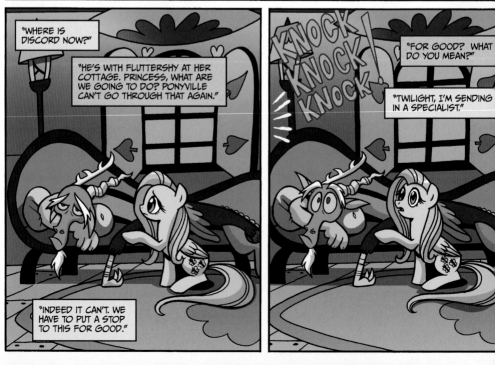

"WHERE IS DISCORD NOW?"

"HE'S WITH FLUTTERSHY AT HER COTTAGE. PRINCESS, WHAT ARE WE GOING TO DO? PONYVILLE CAN'T GO THROUGH THAT AGAIN."

"INDEED IT CAN'T. WE HAVE TO PUT A STOP TO THIS FOR GOOD."

KNOCK KNOCK KNOCK!

"FOR GOOD? WHAT DO YOU MEAN?"

"TWILIGHT, I'M SENDING IN A SPECIALIST."

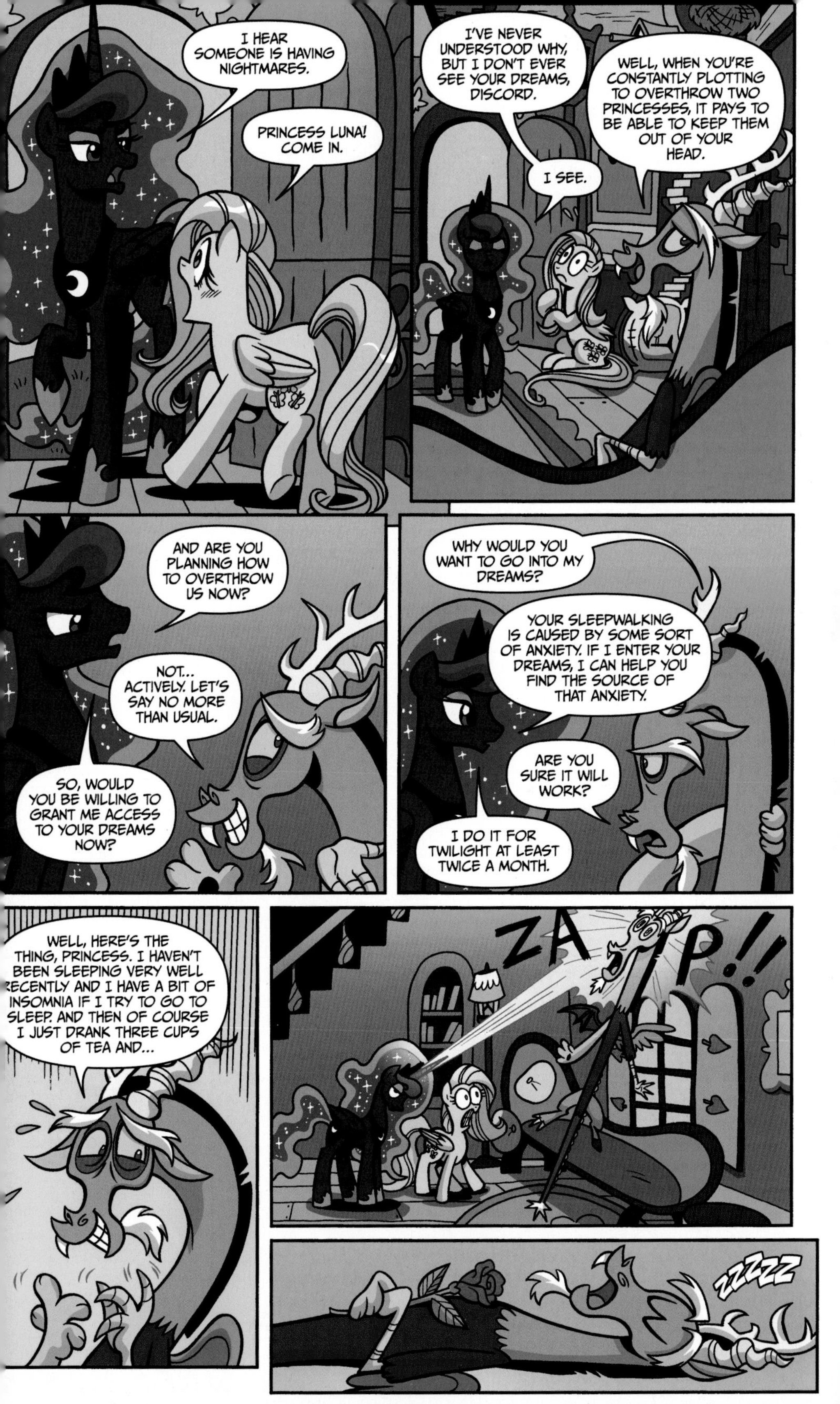
I HEAR SOMEONE IS HAVING NIGHTMARES.
PRINCESS LUNA! COME IN.
I'VE NEVER UNDERSTOOD WHY, BUT I DON'T EVER SEE YOUR DREAMS, DISCORD.
I SEE.
WELL, WHEN YOU'RE CONSTANTLY PLOTTING TO OVERTHROW TWO PRINCESSES, IT PAYS TO BE ABLE TO KEEP THEM OUT OF YOUR HEAD.
AND ARE YOU PLANNING HOW TO OVERTHROW US NOW?
NOT... ACTIVELY. LET'S SAY NO MORE THAN USUAL.
SO, WOULD YOU BE WILLING TO GRANT ME ACCESS TO YOUR DREAMS NOW?
WHY WOULD YOU WANT TO GO INTO MY DREAMS?
YOUR SLEEPWALKING IS CAUSED BY SOME SORT OF ANXIETY. IF I ENTER YOUR DREAMS, I CAN HELP YOU FIND THE SOURCE OF THAT ANXIETY.
ARE YOU SURE IT WILL WORK?
I DO IT FOR TWILIGHT AT LEAST TWICE A MONTH.
WELL, HERE'S THE THING, PRINCESS. I HAVEN'T BEEN SLEEPING VERY WELL RECENTLY AND I HAVE A BIT OF INSOMNIA IF I TRY TO GO TO SLEEP. AND THEN OF COURSE I JUST DRANK THREE CUPS OF TEA AND...
ZAP!!
ZZZZZ

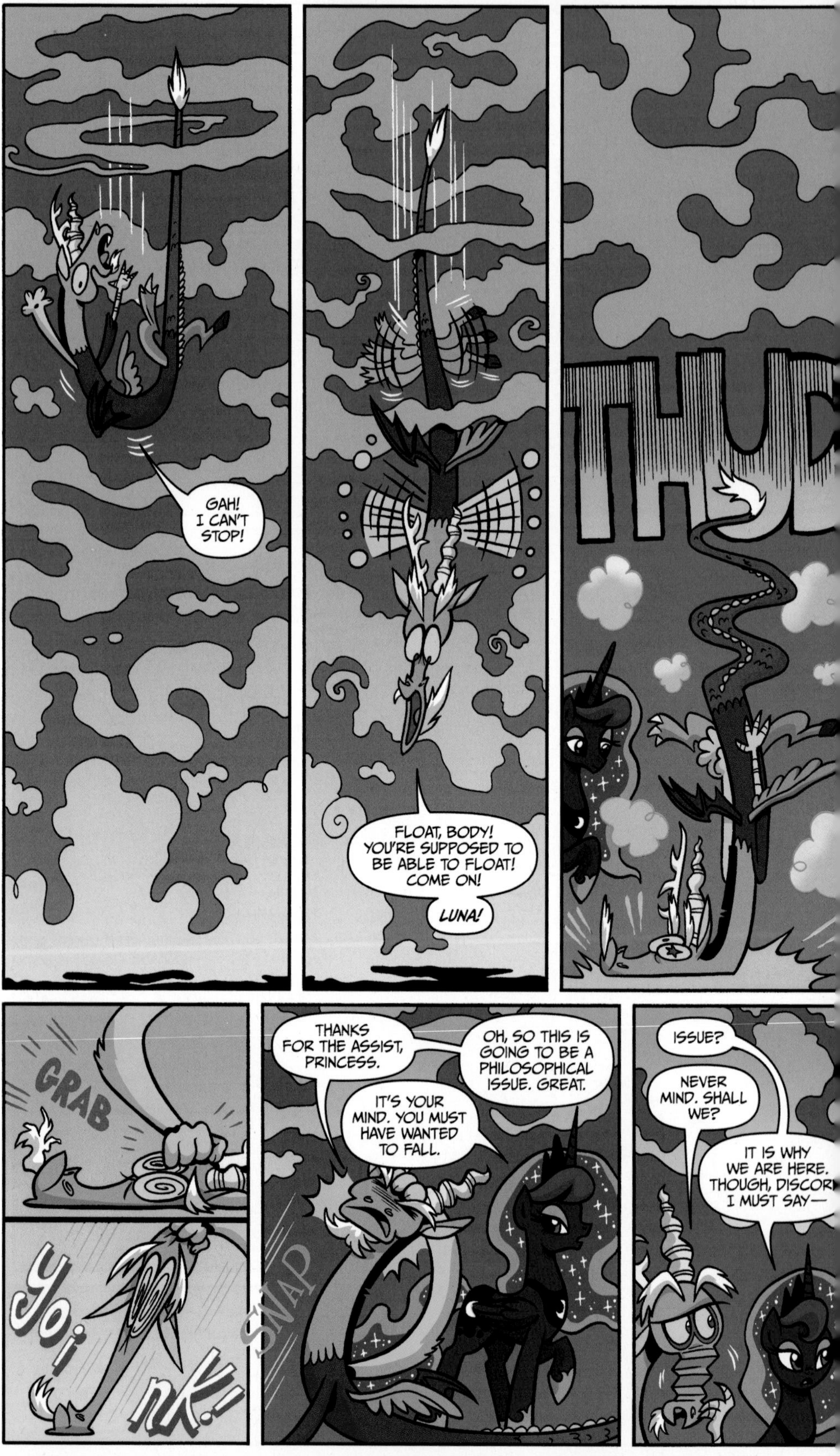
GAH! I CAN'T STOP!
FLOAT, BODY! YOU'RE SUPPOSED TO BE ABLE TO FLOAT! COME ON!
LUNA!
THUD
GRAB
Yoink!
SNAP
THANKS FOR THE ASSIST, PRINCESS.
IT'S YOUR MIND. YOU MUST HAVE WANTED TO FALL.
OH, SO THIS IS GOING TO BE A PHILOSOPHICAL ISSUE. GREAT.
ISSUE?
NEVER MIND. SHALL WE?
IT IS WHY WE ARE HERE. THOUGH, DISCOR
I MUST SAY—

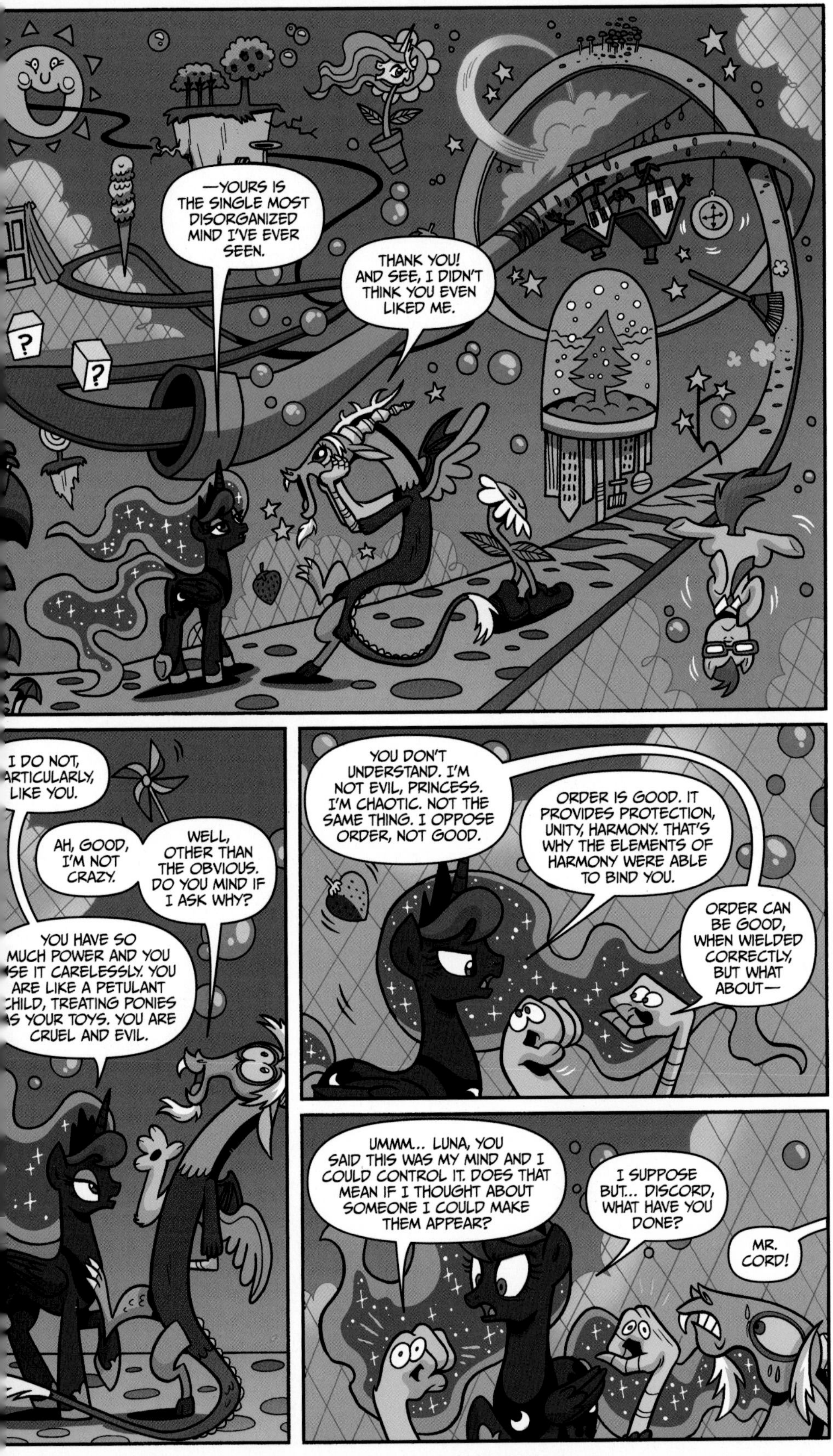
—YOURS IS THE SINGLE MOST DISORGANIZED MIND I'VE EVER SEEN.
THANK YOU! AND SEE, I DIDN'T THINK YOU EVEN LIKED ME.
I DO NOT, ARTICULARLY, LIKE YOU.
AH, GOOD, I'M NOT CRAZY.
WELL, OTHER THAN THE OBVIOUS. DO YOU MIND IF I ASK WHY?
YOU HAVE SO MUCH POWER AND YOU SE IT CARELESSLY. YOU ARE LIKE A PETULANT CHILD, TREATING PONIES S YOUR TOYS. YOU ARE CRUEL AND EVIL.
YOU DON'T UNDERSTAND. I'M NOT EVIL, PRINCESS. I'M CHAOTIC. NOT THE SAME THING. I OPPOSE ORDER, NOT GOOD.
ORDER IS GOOD. IT PROVIDES PROTECTION, UNITY, HARMONY. THAT'S WHY THE ELEMENTS OF HARMONY WERE ABLE TO BIND YOU.
ORDER CAN BE GOOD, WHEN WIELDED CORRECTLY, BUT WHAT ABOUT—
UMMM... LUNA, YOU SAID THIS WAS MY MIND AND I COULD CONTROL IT. DOES THAT MEAN IF I THOUGHT ABOUT SOMEONE I COULD MAKE THEM APPEAR?
I SUPPOSE BUT... DISCORD, WHAT HAVE YOU DONE?
MR. CORD!

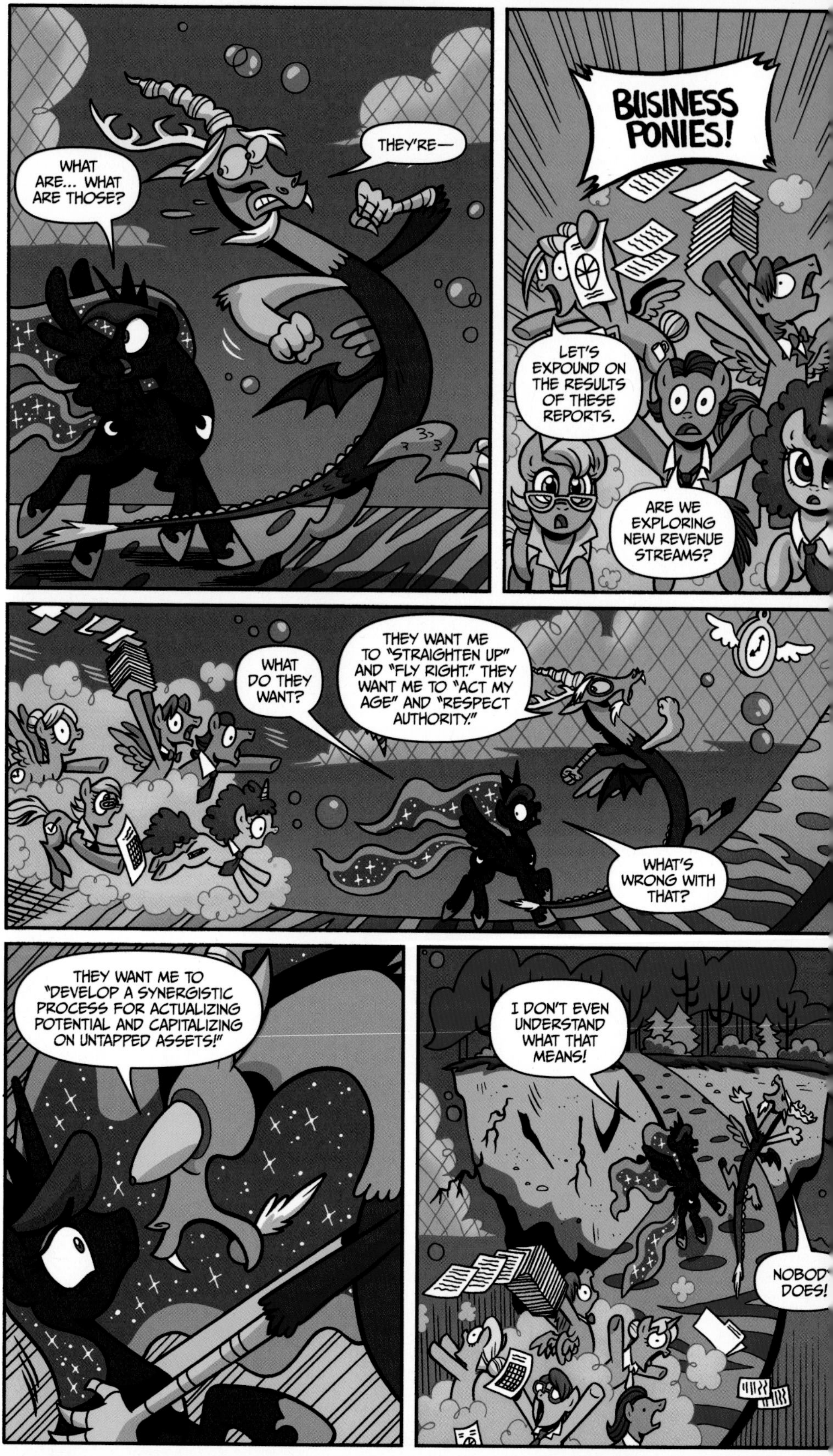
WHAT ARE... WHAT ARE THOSE?
THEY'RE—
BUSINESS PONIES!
LET'S EXPOUND ON THE RESULTS OF THESE REPORTS.
ARE WE EXPLORING NEW REVENUE STREAMS?
WHAT DO THEY WANT?
THEY WANT ME TO "STRAIGHTEN UP" AND "FLY RIGHT." THEY WANT ME TO "ACT MY AGE" AND "RESPECT AUTHORITY."
WHAT'S WRONG WITH THAT?
THEY WANT ME TO "DEVELOP A SYNERGISTIC PROCESS FOR ACTUALIZING POTENTIAL AND CAPITALIZING ON UNTAPPED ASSETS!"
I DON'T EVEN UNDERSTAND WHAT THAT MEANS!
NOBOD DOES!

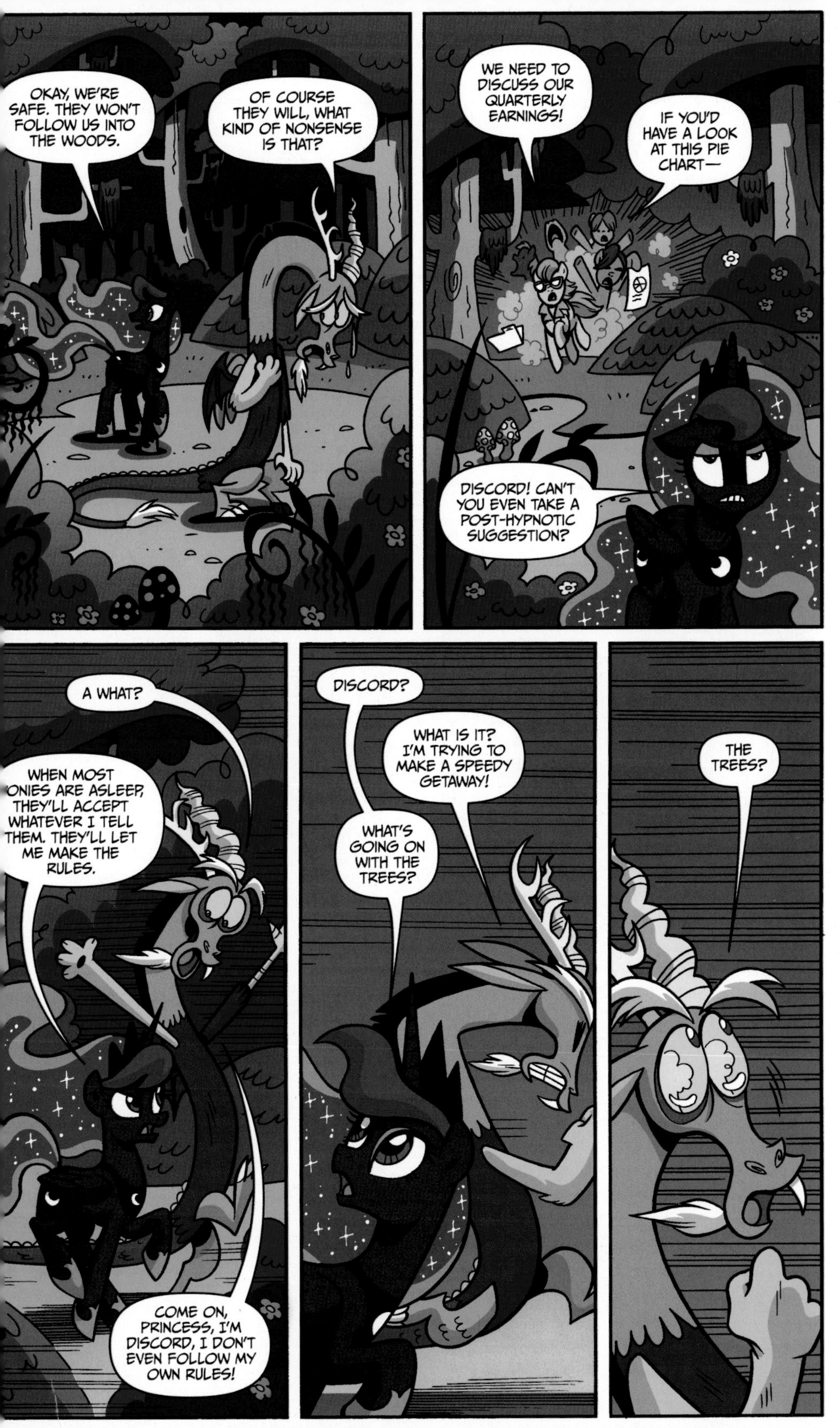
OKAY, WE'RE SAFE. THEY WON'T FOLLOW US INTO THE WOODS.
OF COURSE THEY WILL, WHAT KIND OF NONSENSE IS THAT?
WE NEED TO DISCUSS OUR QUARTERLY EARNINGS!
IF YOU'D HAVE A LOOK AT THIS PIE CHART—
DISCORD! CAN'T YOU EVEN TAKE A POST-HYPNOTIC SUGGESTION?
A WHAT?
WHEN MOST PONIES ARE ASLEEP, THEY'LL ACCEPT WHATEVER I TELL THEM. THEY'LL LET ME MAKE THE RULES.
COME ON, PRINCESS, I'M DISCORD, I DON'T EVEN FOLLOW MY OWN RULES!
DISCORD?
WHAT IS IT? I'M TRYING TO MAKE A SPEEDY GETAWAY!
WHAT'S GOING ON WITH THE TREES?
THE TREES?

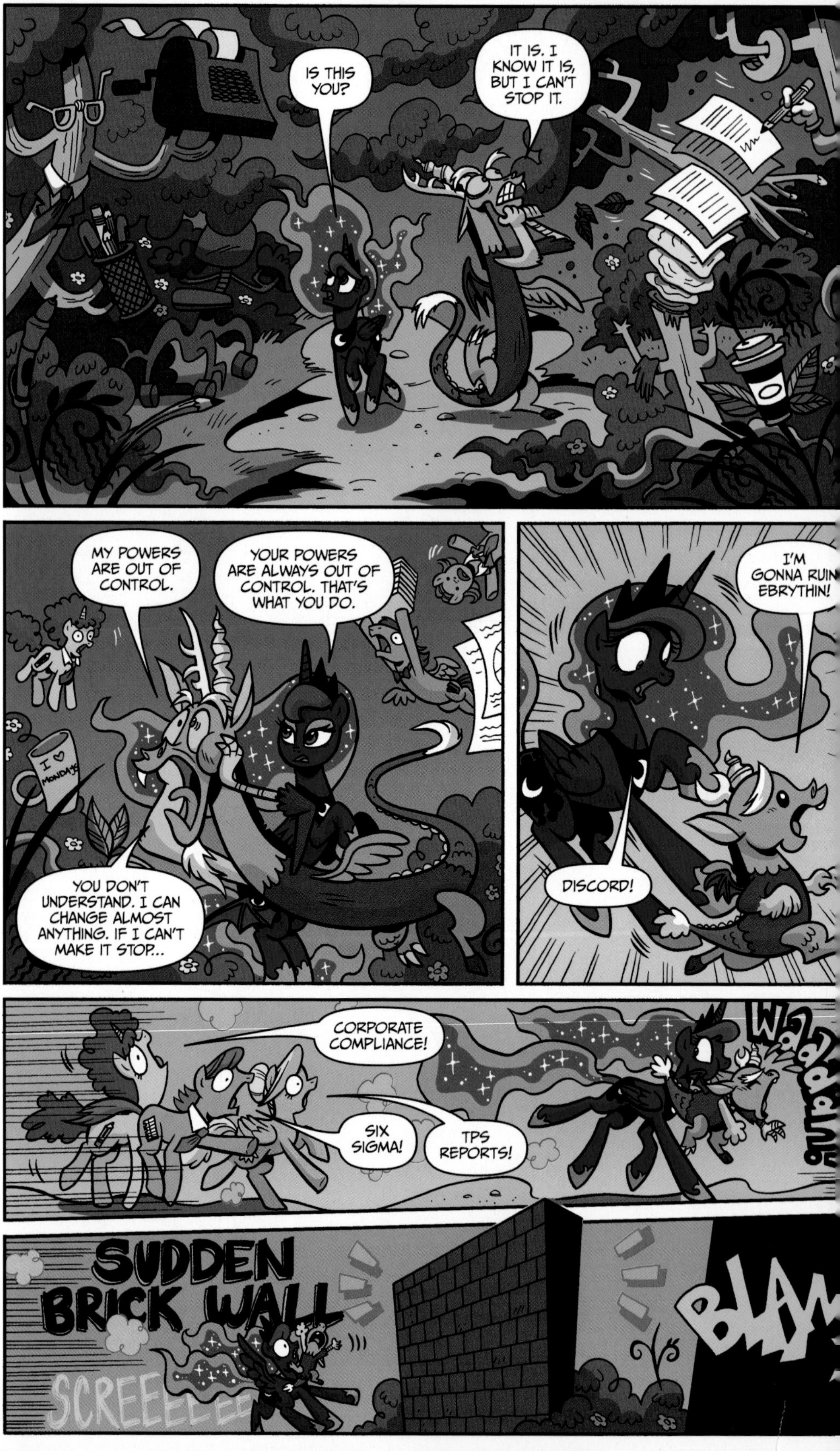
IS THIS YOU?
IT IS. I KNOW IT IS, BUT I CAN'T STOP IT.
MY POWERS ARE OUT OF CONTROL.
YOUR POWERS ARE ALWAYS OUT OF CONTROL. THAT'S WHAT YOU DO.
YOU DON'T UNDERSTAND. I CAN CHANGE ALMOST ANYTHING. IF I CAN'T MAKE IT STOP...
I ♡ MONDAYS
I'M GONNA RUIN EBRYTHIN!
DISCORD!
CORPORATE COMPLIANCE!
SIX SIGMA!
TPS REPORTS!
SUDDEN BRICK WALL
SCREEEEEE

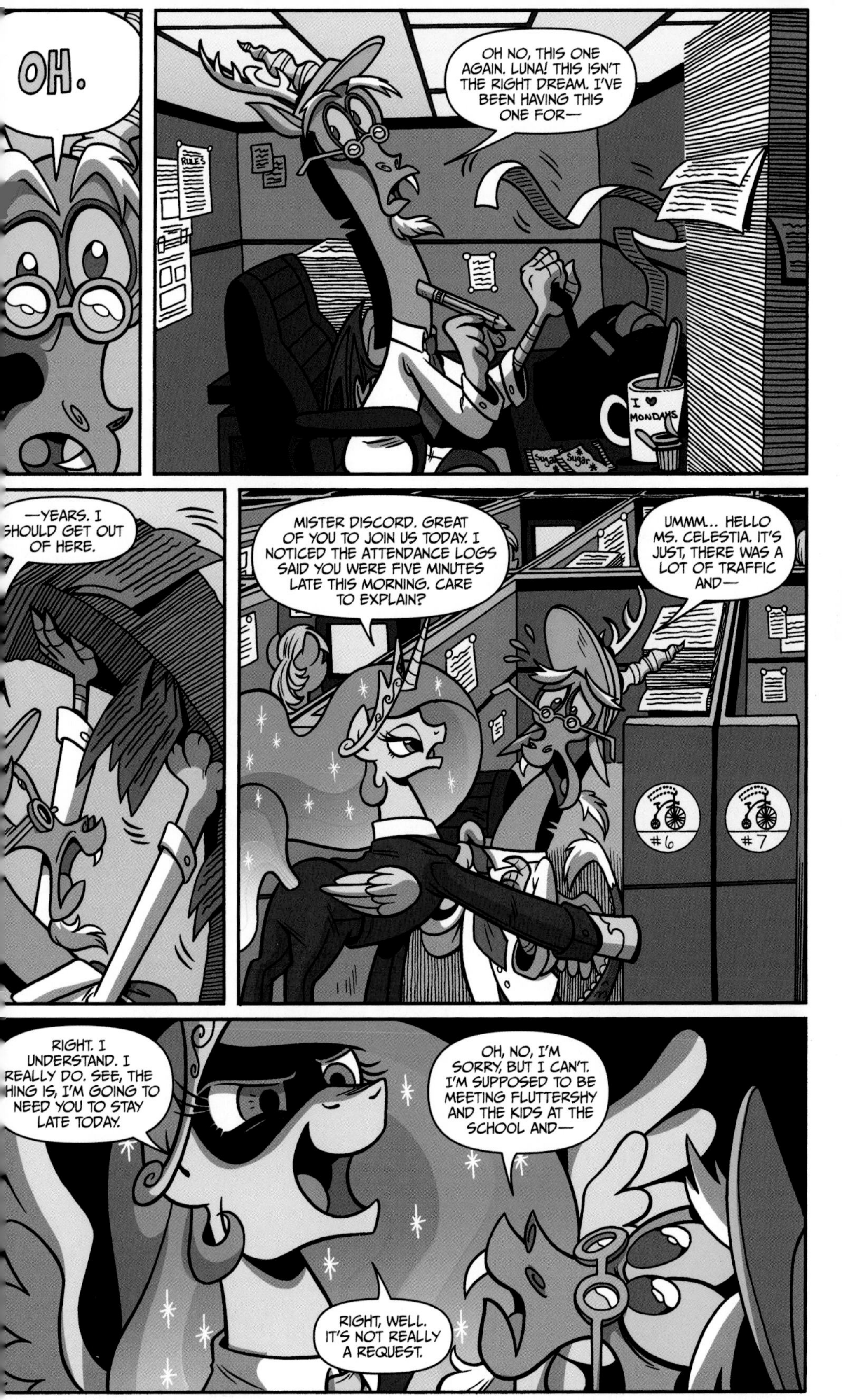
OH.
OH NO, THIS ONE AGAIN. LUNA! THIS ISN'T THE RIGHT DREAM. I'VE BEEN HAVING THIS ONE FOR—
RULES
I ♥ MONDAYS
Sugar
Sugar
—YEARS. I SHOULD GET OUT OF HERE.
MISTER DISCORD. GREAT OF YOU TO JOIN US TODAY. I NOTICED THE ATTENDANCE LOGS SAID YOU WERE FIVE MINUTES LATE THIS MORNING. CARE TO EXPLAIN?
UMMM... HELLO MS. CELESTIA. IT'S JUST, THERE WAS A LOT OF TRAFFIC AND—
#6
#7
RIGHT. I UNDERSTAND. I REALLY DO. SEE, THE THING IS, I'M GOING TO NEED YOU TO STAY LATE TODAY.
OH, NO, I'M SORRY, BUT I CAN'T. I'M SUPPOSED TO BE MEETING FLUTTERSHY AND THE KIDS AT THE SCHOOL AND—
RIGHT, WELL. IT'S NOT REALLY A REQUEST.

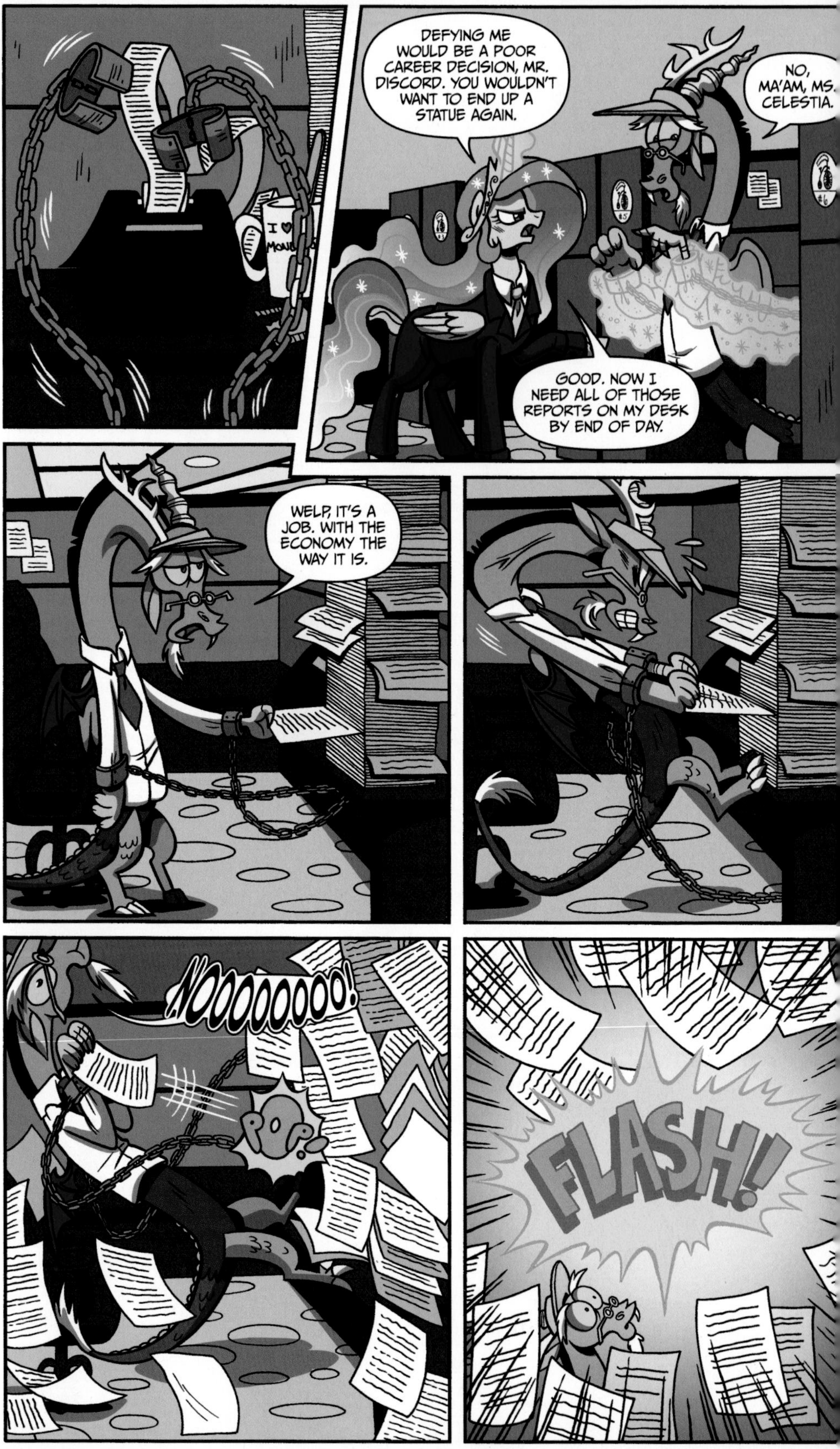
DEFYING ME WOULD BE A POOR CAREER DECISION, MR. DISCORD. YOU WOULDN'T WANT TO END UP A STATUE AGAIN.
NO, MA'AM, MS. CELESTIA.
GOOD. NOW I NEED ALL OF THOSE REPORTS ON MY DESK BY END OF DAY.
WELP, IT'S A JOB. WITH THE ECONOMY THE WAY IT IS.
NOOOOOOOO!
POP!
FLASH!

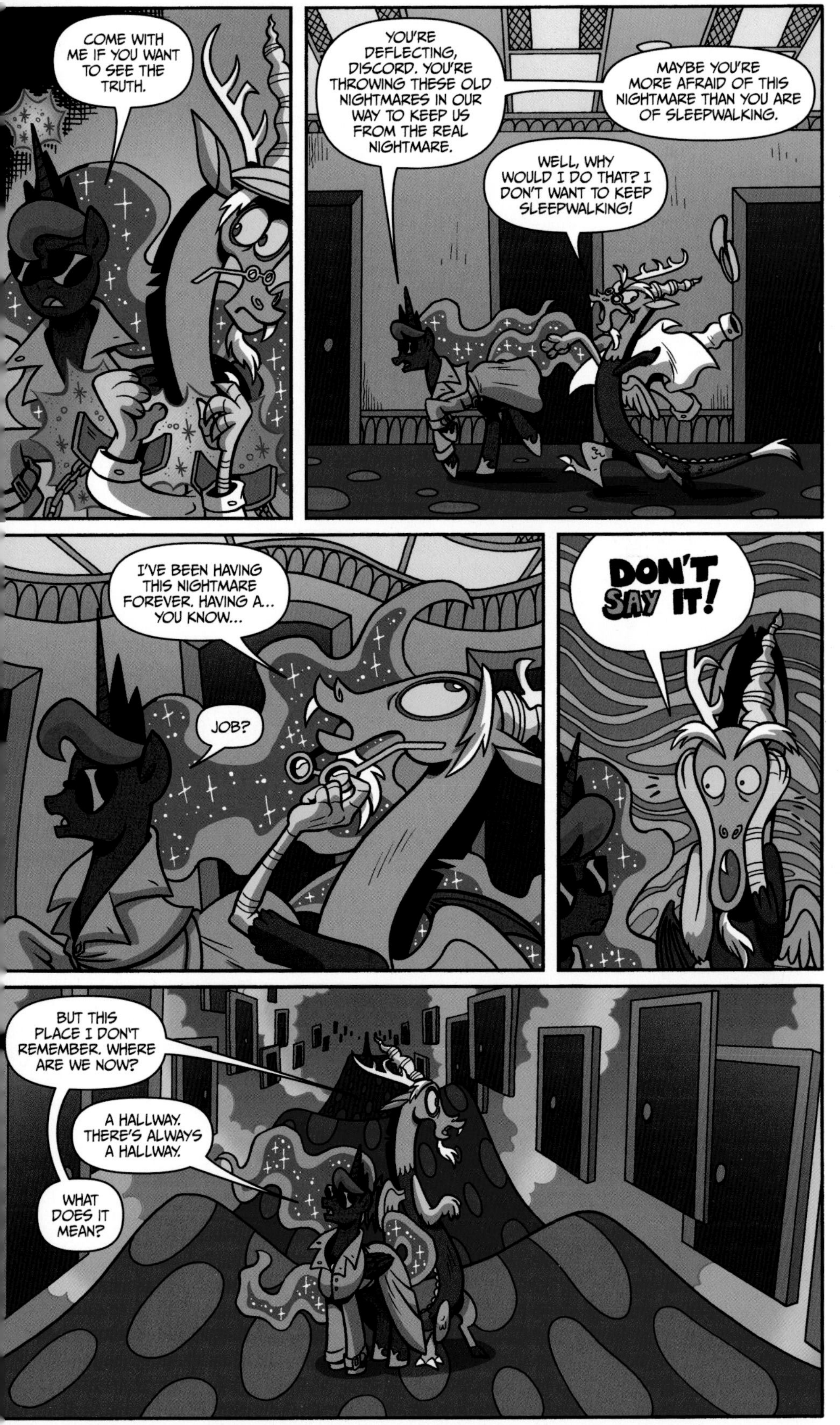
COME WITH ME IF YOU WANT TO SEE THE TRUTH.
YOU'RE DEFLECTING, DISCORD. YOU'RE THROWING THESE OLD NIGHTMARES IN OUR WAY TO KEEP US FROM THE REAL NIGHTMARE.
MAYBE YOU'RE MORE AFRAID OF THIS NIGHTMARE THAN YOU ARE OF SLEEPWALKING.
WELL, WHY WOULD I DO THAT? I DON'T WANT TO KEEP SLEEPWALKING!
I'VE BEEN HAVING THIS NIGHTMARE FOREVER. HAVING A... YOU KNOW...
JOB?
DON'T SAY IT!
BUT THIS PLACE I DON'T REMEMBER. WHERE ARE WE NOW?
A HALLWAY. THERE'S ALWAYS A HALLWAY.
WHAT DOES IT MEAN?

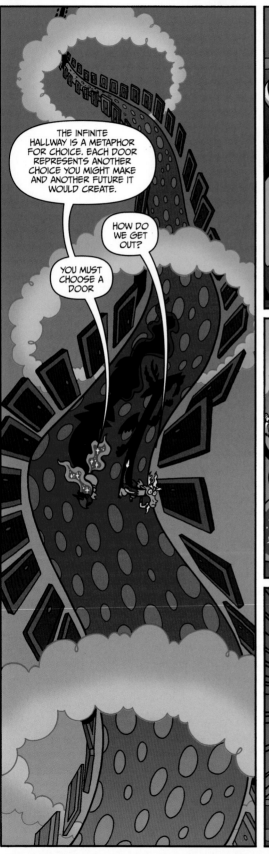

THE INFINITE HALLWAY IS A METAPHOR FOR CHOICE. EACH DOOR REPRESENTS ANOTHER CHOICE YOU MIGHT MAKE AND ANOTHER FUTURE IT WOULD CREATE.

HOW DO WE GET OUT?

YOU MUST CHOOSE A DOOR

THIS ONE HAS DIAMONDS. THAT MUST BE A GOOD SIGN, RIGHT?

THAT HARDLY SEEMS LIKE THE BEST BASIS TO CHOOSE.

WHAT ABOUT THIS ONE? IT LOOKS IMPORTANT.

NONSENSE, THIS IS CLEARLY THE BEST CHOICE.

CAUTION CAUTION CAUT

STOP

CAUTION CAUTION CAUTION CAUTI

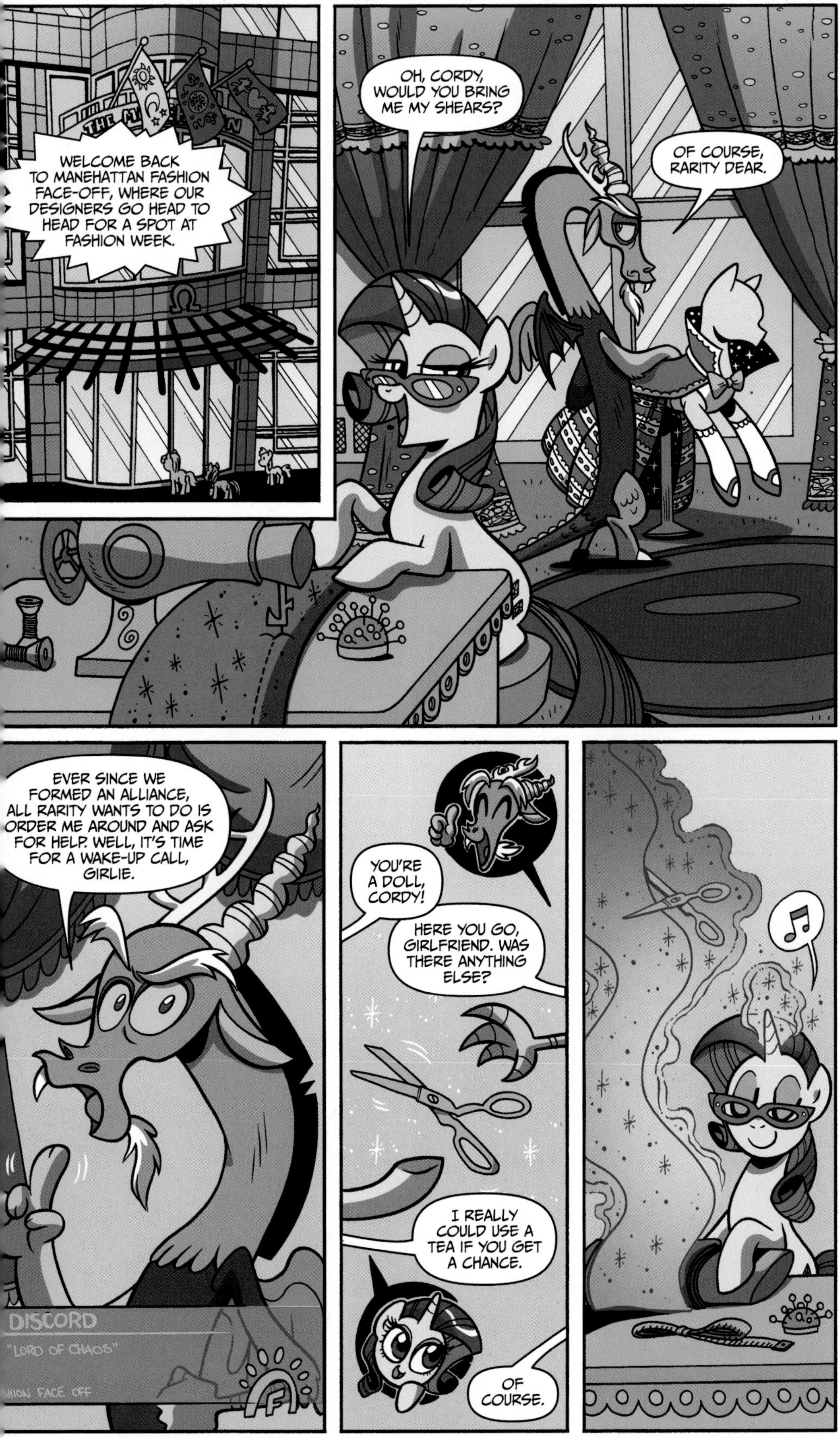
WELCOME BACK TO MANEHATTAN FASHION FACE-OFF, WHERE OUR DESIGNERS GO HEAD TO HEAD FOR A SPOT AT FASHION WEEK.
OH, CORDY, WOULD YOU BRING ME MY SHEARS?
OF COURSE, RARITY DEAR.
EVER SINCE WE FORMED AN ALLIANCE, ALL RARITY WANTS TO DO IS ORDER ME AROUND AND ASK FOR HELP. WELL, IT'S TIME FOR A WAKE-UP CALL, GIRLIE.
DISCORD
"LORD OF CHAOS"
FACE OFF
YOU'RE A DOLL, CORDY!
HERE YOU GO, GIRLFRIEND. WAS THERE ANYTHING ELSE?
I REALLY COULD USE A TEA IF YOU GET A CHANCE.
OF COURSE.

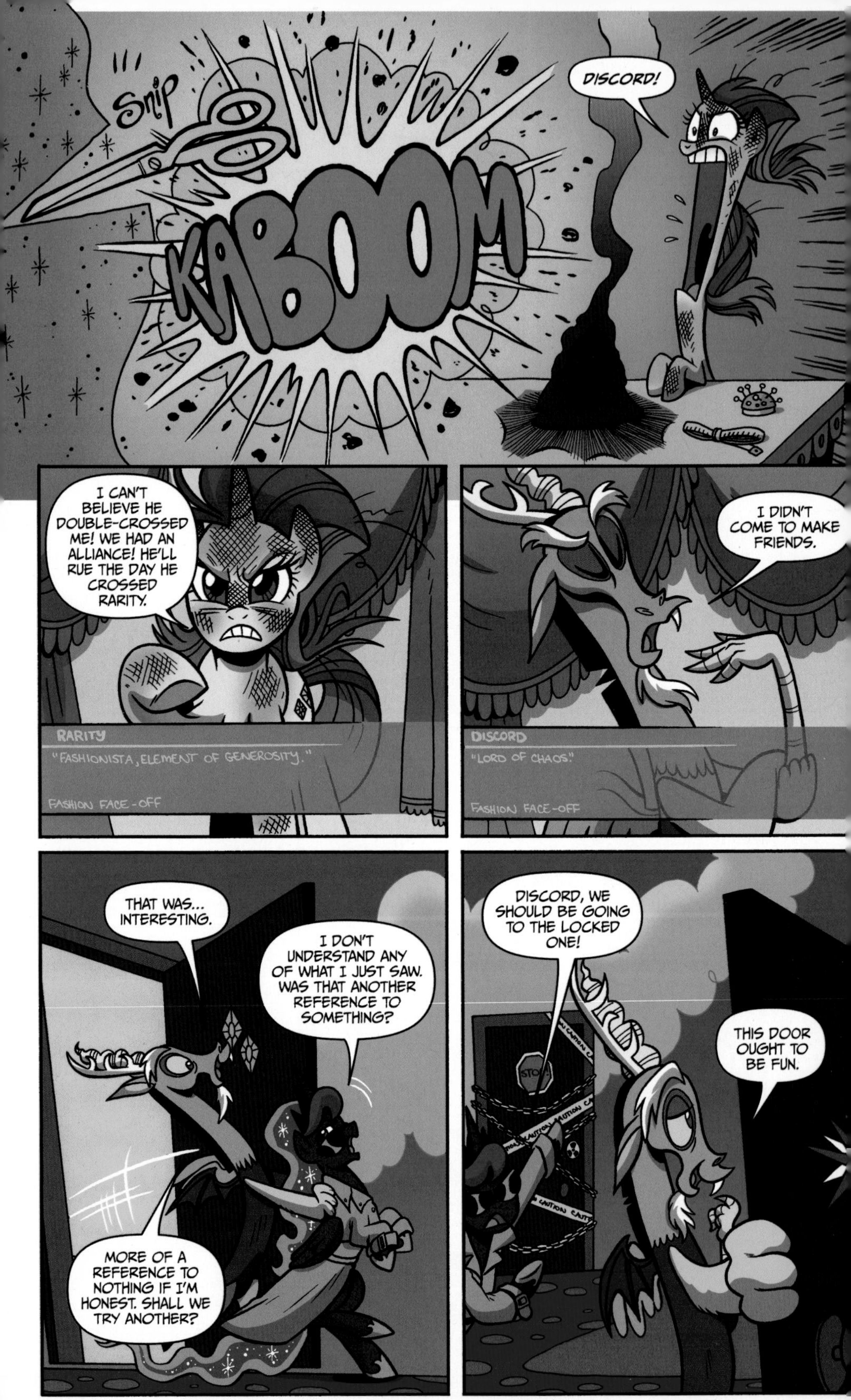

Snip
KABOOM
DISCORD!
I CAN'T BELIEVE HE DOUBLE-CROSSED ME! WE HAD AN ALLIANCE! HE'LL RUE THE DAY HE CROSSED RARITY.
RARITY
"FASHIONISTA, ELEMENT OF GENEROSITY."
FASHION FACE-OFF
I DIDN'T COME TO MAKE FRIENDS.
DISCORD
"LORD OF CHAOS."
FASHION FACE-OFF
THAT WAS... INTERESTING.
I DON'T UNDERSTAND ANY OF WHAT I JUST SAW. WAS THAT ANOTHER REFERENCE TO SOMETHING?
MORE OF A REFERENCE TO NOTHING IF I'M HONEST. SHALL WE TRY ANOTHER?
DISCORD, WE SHOULD BE GOING TO THE LOCKED ONE!
STOP
CAUTION
THIS DOOR OUGHT TO BE FUN.

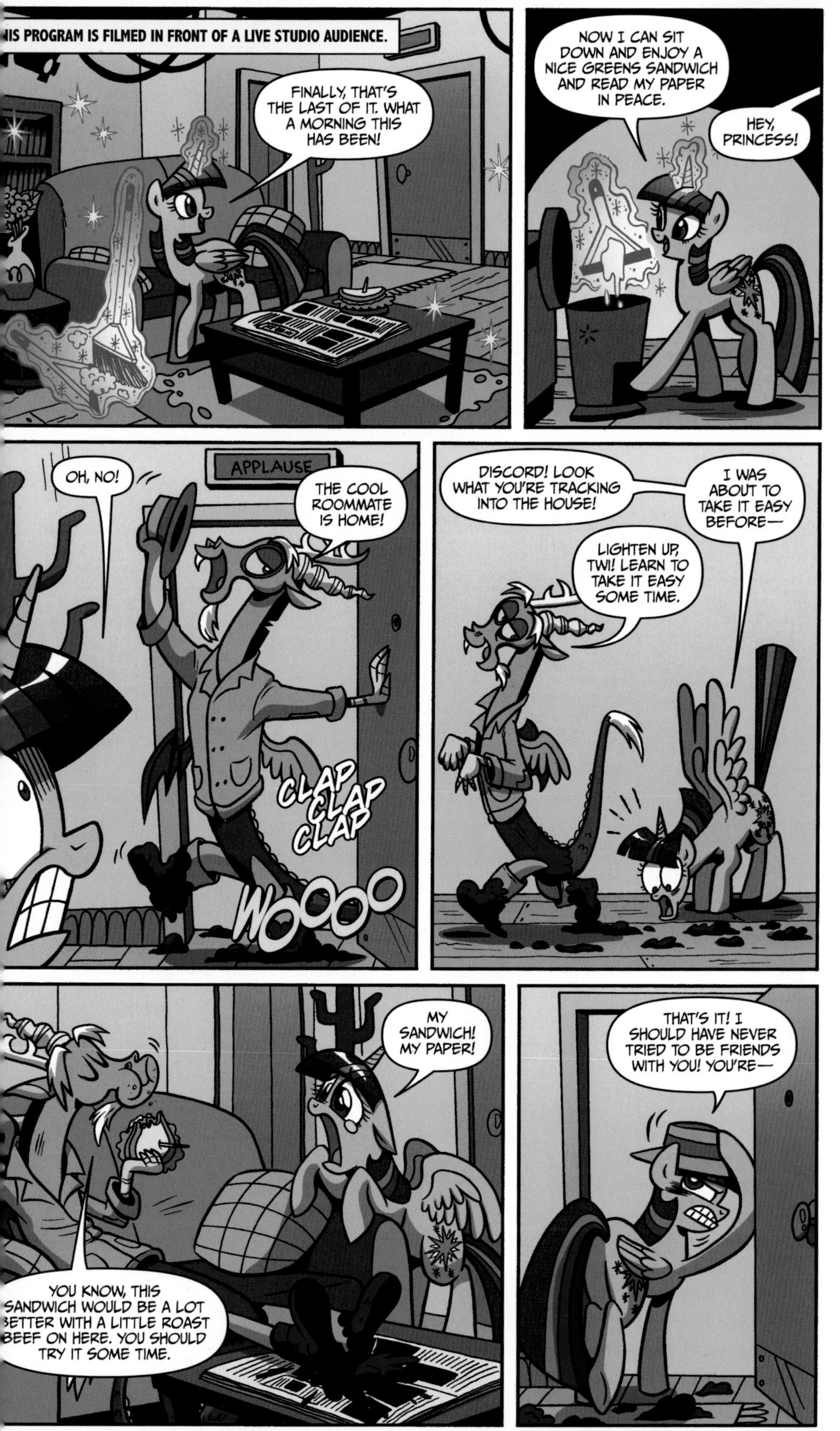
IS PROGRAM IS FILMED IN FRONT OF A LIVE STUDIO AUDIENCE.
FINALLY, THAT'S THE LAST OF IT. WHAT A MORNING THIS HAS BEEN!
NOW I CAN SIT DOWN AND ENJOY A NICE GREENS SANDWICH AND READ MY PAPER IN PEACE.
HEY, PRINCESS!
APPLAUSE
OH, NO!
THE COOL ROOMMATE IS HOME!
CLAP CLAP CLAP
WOOOO
DISCORD! LOOK WHAT YOU'RE TRACKING INTO THE HOUSE!
I WAS ABOUT TO TAKE IT EASY BEFORE—
LIGHTEN UP, TWI! LEARN TO TAKE IT EASY SOME TIME.
MY SANDWICH! MY PAPER!
YOU KNOW, THIS SANDWICH WOULD BE A LOT BETTER WITH A LITTLE ROAST BEEF ON HERE. YOU SHOULD TRY IT SOME TIME.
THAT'S IT! I SHOULD HAVE NEVER TRIED TO BE FRIENDS WITH YOU! YOU'RE—

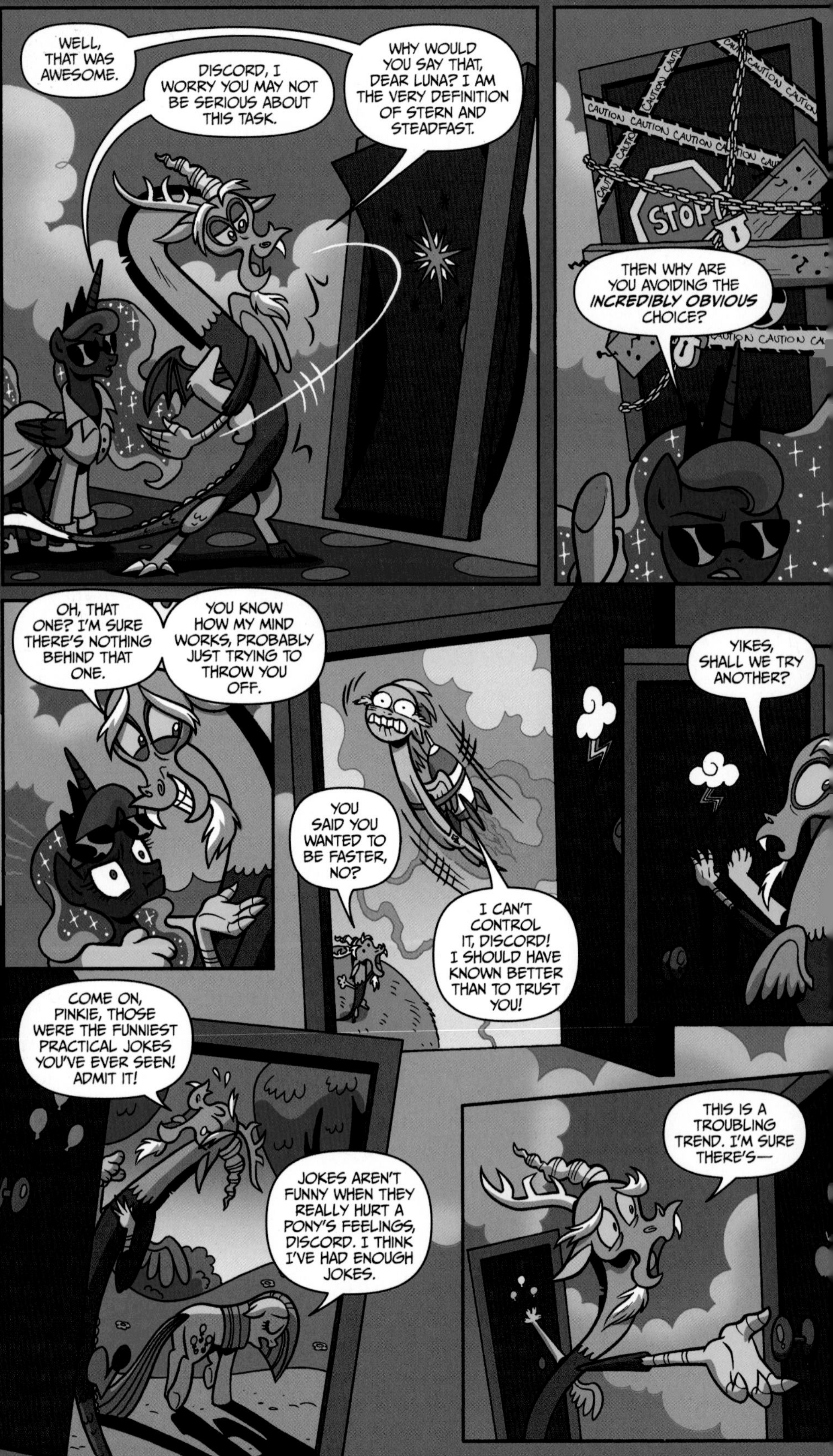
WELL, THAT WAS AWESOME.
DISCORD, I WORRY YOU MAY NOT BE SERIOUS ABOUT THIS TASK.
WHY WOULD YOU SAY THAT, DEAR LUNA? I AM THE VERY DEFINITION OF STERN AND STEADFAST.
CAUTION CAUTION CAUTION
STOP
THEN WHY ARE YOU AVOIDING THE *INCREDIBLY OBVIOUS* CHOICE?
OH, THAT ONE? I'M SURE THERE'S NOTHING BEHIND THAT ONE.
YOU KNOW HOW MY MIND WORKS, PROBABLY JUST TRYING TO THROW YOU OFF.
YOU SAID YOU WANTED TO BE FASTER, NO?
I CAN'T CONTROL IT, DISCORD! I SHOULD HAVE KNOWN BETTER THAN TO TRUST YOU!
YIKES, SHALL WE TRY ANOTHER?
COME ON, PINKIE, THOSE WERE THE FUNNIEST PRACTICAL JOKES YOU'VE EVER SEEN! ADMIT IT!
JOKES AREN'T FUNNY WHEN THEY REALLY HURT A PONY'S FEELINGS, DISCORD. I THINK I'VE HAD ENOUGH JOKES.
THIS IS A TROUBLING TREND. I'M SURE THERE'S—

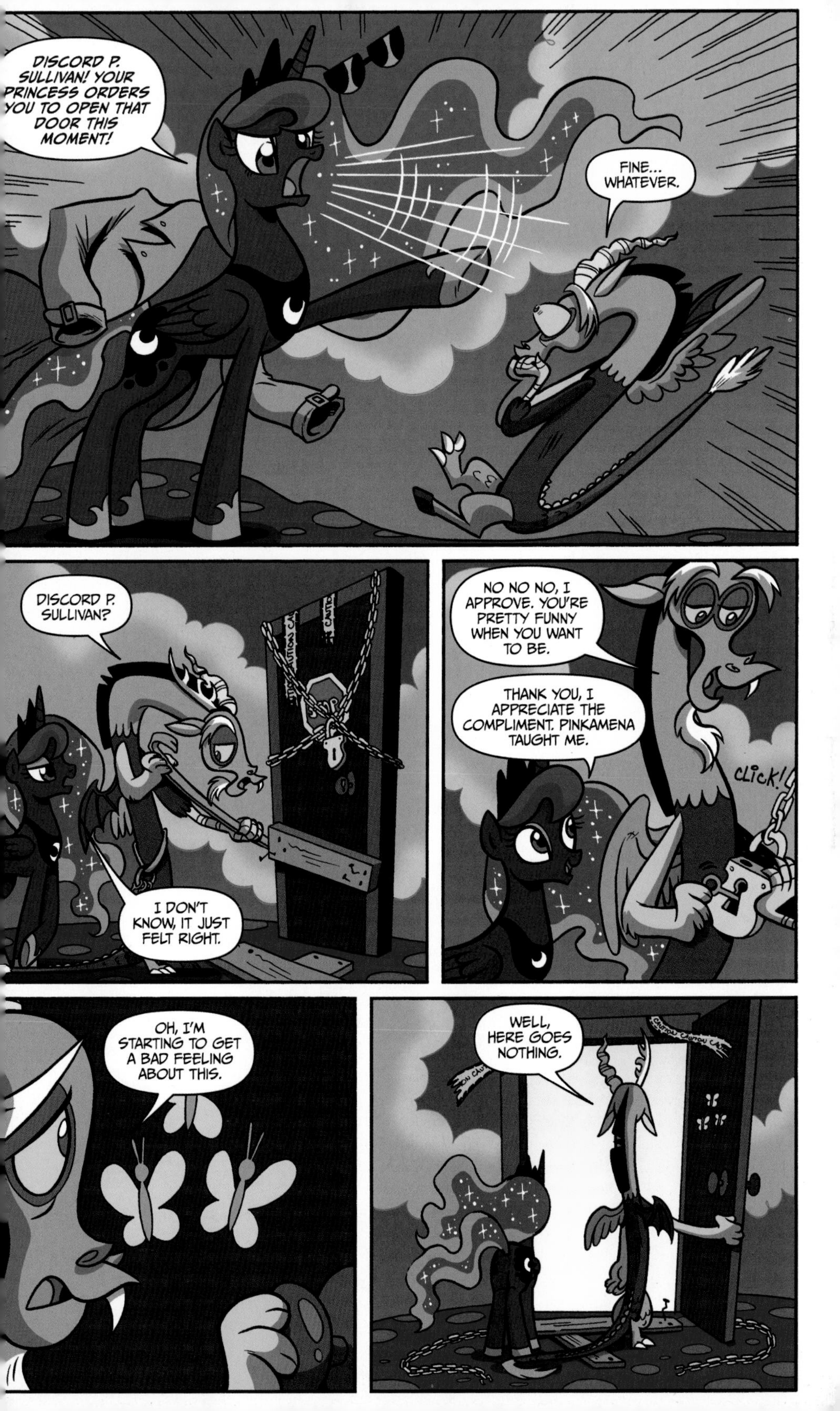
DISCORD P. SULLIVAN! YOUR PRINCESS ORDERS YOU TO OPEN THAT DOOR THIS MOMENT!
FINE... WHATEVER.
DISCORD P. SULLIVAN?
I DON'T KNOW, IT JUST FELT RIGHT.
NO NO NO, I APPROVE. YOU'RE PRETTY FUNNY WHEN YOU WANT TO BE.
THANK YOU, I APPRECIATE THE COMPLIMENT. PINKAMENA TAUGHT ME.
CLICK!
OH, I'M STARTING TO GET A BAD FEELING ABOUT THIS.
WELL, HERE GOES NOTHING.

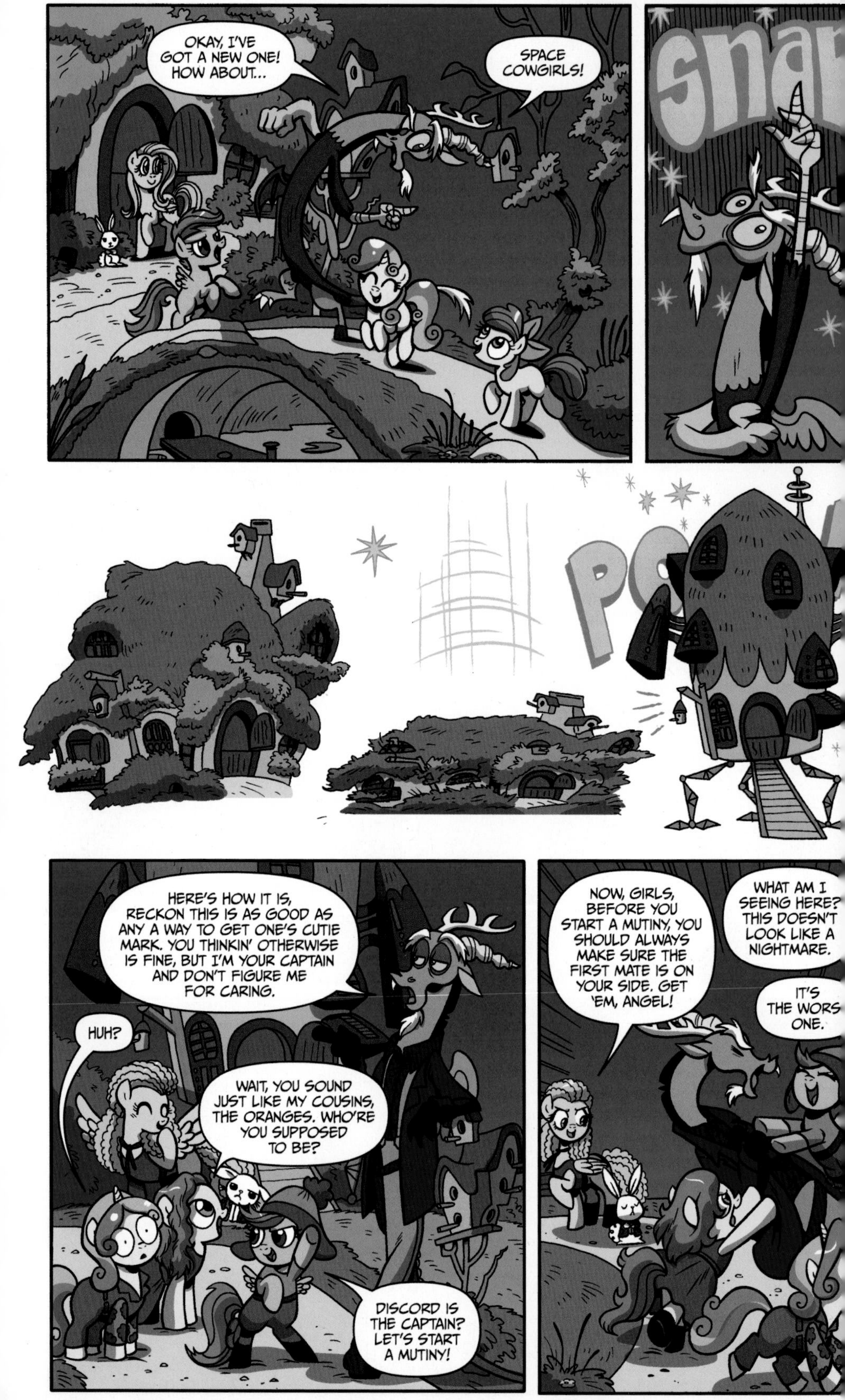
OKAY, I'VE GOT A NEW ONE! HOW ABOUT...
SPACE COWGIRLS!
HERE'S HOW IT IS, RECKON THIS IS AS GOOD AS ANY A WAY TO GET ONE'S CUTIE MARK. YOU THINKIN' OTHERWISE IS FINE, BUT I'M YOUR CAPTAIN AND DON'T FIGURE ME FOR CARING.
HUH?
WAIT, YOU SOUND JUST LIKE MY COUSINS, THE ORANGES. WHO'RE YOU SUPPOSED TO BE?
DISCORD IS THE CAPTAIN? LET'S START A MUTINY!
NOW, GIRLS, BEFORE YOU START A MUTINY, YOU SHOULD ALWAYS MAKE SURE THE FIRST MATE IS ON YOUR SIDE. GET 'EM, ANGEL!
WHAT AM I SEEING HERE? THIS DOESN'T LOOK LIKE A NIGHTMARE.

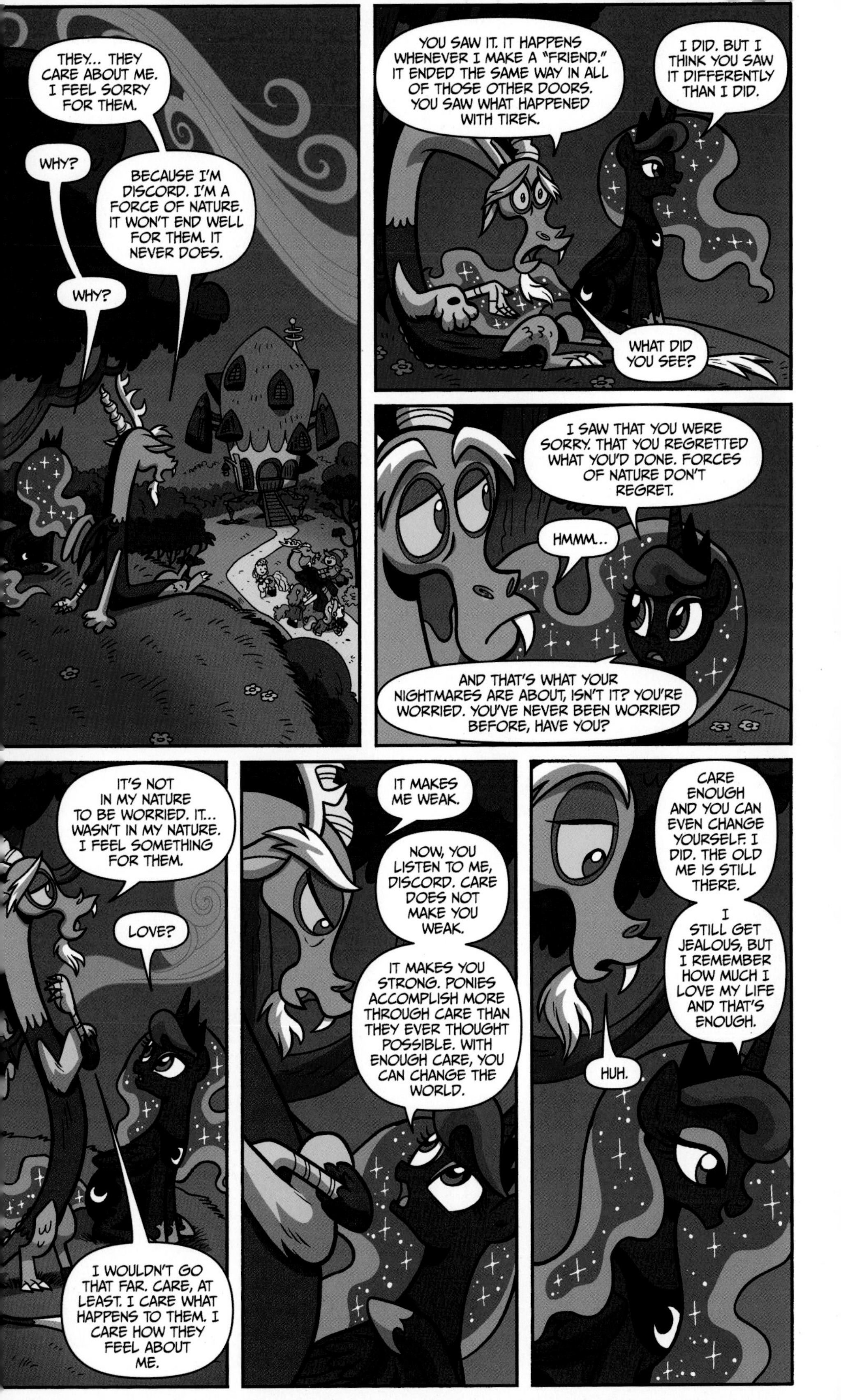
THEY... THEY CARE ABOUT ME. I FEEL SORRY FOR THEM.
WHY?
BECAUSE I'M DISCORD. I'M A FORCE OF NATURE. IT WON'T END WELL FOR THEM. IT NEVER DOES.
WHY?
YOU SAW IT. IT HAPPENS WHENEVER I MAKE A "FRIEND." IT ENDED THE SAME WAY IN ALL OF THOSE OTHER DOORS. YOU SAW WHAT HAPPENED WITH TIREK.
I DID. BUT I THINK YOU SAW IT DIFFERENTLY THAN I DID.
WHAT DID YOU SEE?
I SAW THAT YOU WERE SORRY. THAT YOU REGRETTED WHAT YOU'D DONE. FORCES OF NATURE DON'T REGRET.
HMMM...
AND THAT'S WHAT YOUR NIGHTMARES ARE ABOUT, ISN'T IT? YOU'RE WORRIED. YOU'VE NEVER BEEN WORRIED BEFORE, HAVE YOU?
IT'S NOT IN MY NATURE TO BE WORRIED. IT... WASN'T IN MY NATURE. I FEEL SOMETHING FOR THEM.
LOVE?
I WOULDN'T GO THAT FAR. CARE, AT LEAST. I CARE WHAT HAPPENS TO THEM. I CARE HOW THEY FEEL ABOUT ME.
IT MAKES ME WEAK.
NOW, YOU LISTEN TO ME, DISCORD. CARE DOES NOT MAKE YOU WEAK.
IT MAKES YOU STRONG. PONIES ACCOMPLISH MORE THROUGH CARE THAN THEY EVER THOUGHT POSSIBLE. WITH ENOUGH CARE, YOU CAN CHANGE THE WORLD.
CARE ENOUGH AND YOU CAN EVEN CHANGE YOURSELF. I DID. THE OLD ME IS STILL THERE.
I STILL GET JEALOUS, BUT I REMEMBER HOW MUCH I LOVE MY LIFE AND THAT'S ENOUGH.
HUH.

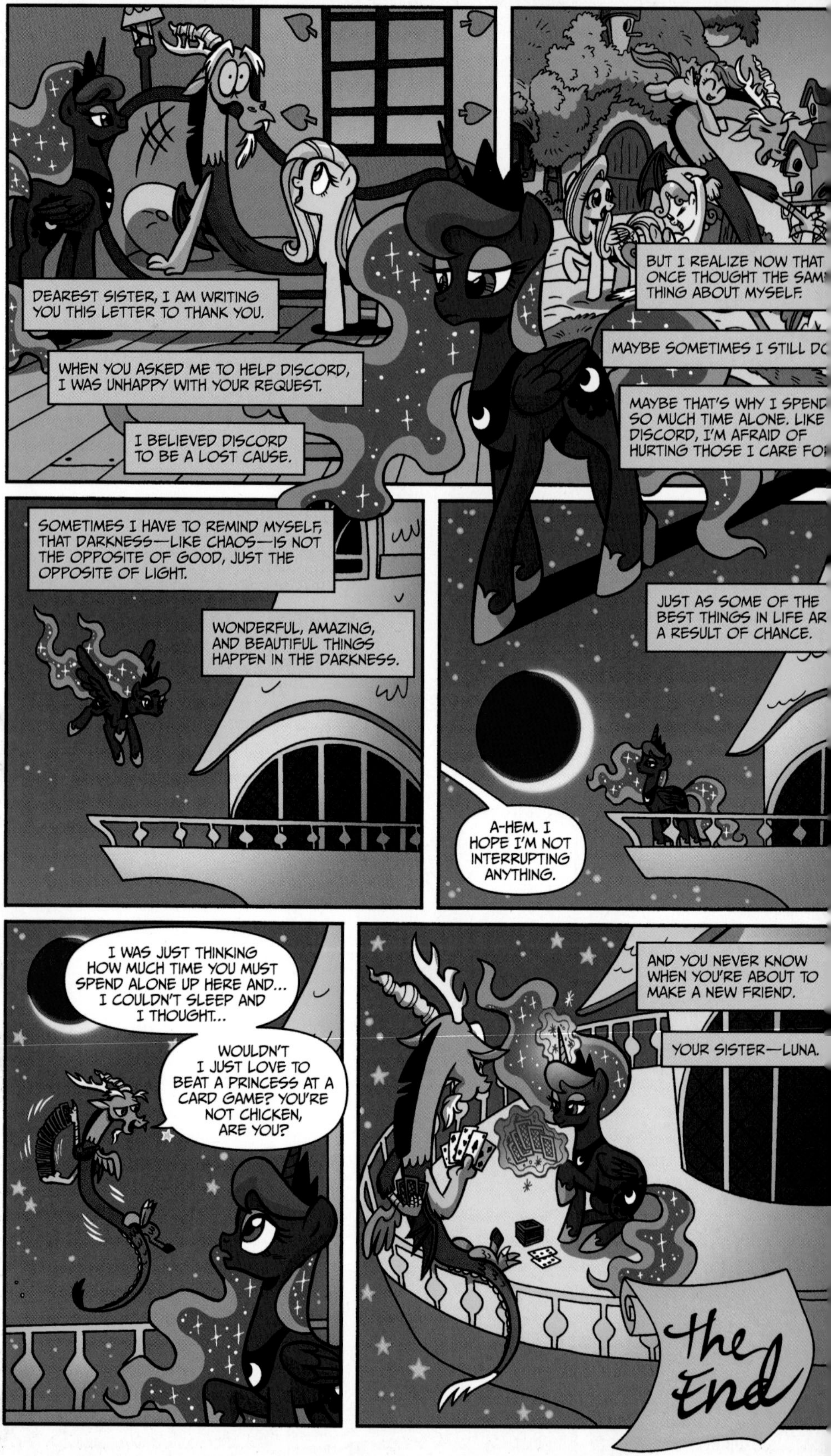
DEAREST SISTER, I AM WRITING YOU THIS LETTER TO THANK YOU.
WHEN YOU ASKED ME TO HELP DISCORD, I WAS UNHAPPY WITH YOUR REQUEST.
I BELIEVED DISCORD TO BE A LOST CAUSE.
BUT I REALIZE NOW THAT I ONCE THOUGHT THE SAM THING ABOUT MYSELF.
MAYBE SOMETIMES I STILL DO
MAYBE THAT'S WHY I SPEND SO MUCH TIME ALONE. LIKE DISCORD, I'M AFRAID OF HURTING THOSE I CARE FO
SOMETIMES I HAVE TO REMIND MYSELF, THAT DARKNESS—LIKE CHAOS—IS NOT THE OPPOSITE OF GOOD, JUST THE OPPOSITE OF LIGHT.
WONDERFUL, AMAZING, AND BEAUTIFUL THINGS HAPPEN IN THE DARKNESS.
JUST AS SOME OF THE BEST THINGS IN LIFE AR A RESULT OF CHANCE.
A-HEM. I HOPE I'M NOT INTERRUPTING ANYTHING.
I WAS JUST THINKING HOW MUCH TIME YOU MUST SPEND ALONE UP HERE AND... I COULDN'T SLEEP AND I THOUGHT...
WOULDN'T I JUST LOVE TO BEAT A PRINCESS AT A CARD GAME? YOU'RE NOT CHICKEN, ARE YOU?
AND YOU NEVER KNOW WHEN YOU'RE ABOUT TO MAKE A NEW FRIEND.
YOUR SISTER—LUNA.
the End

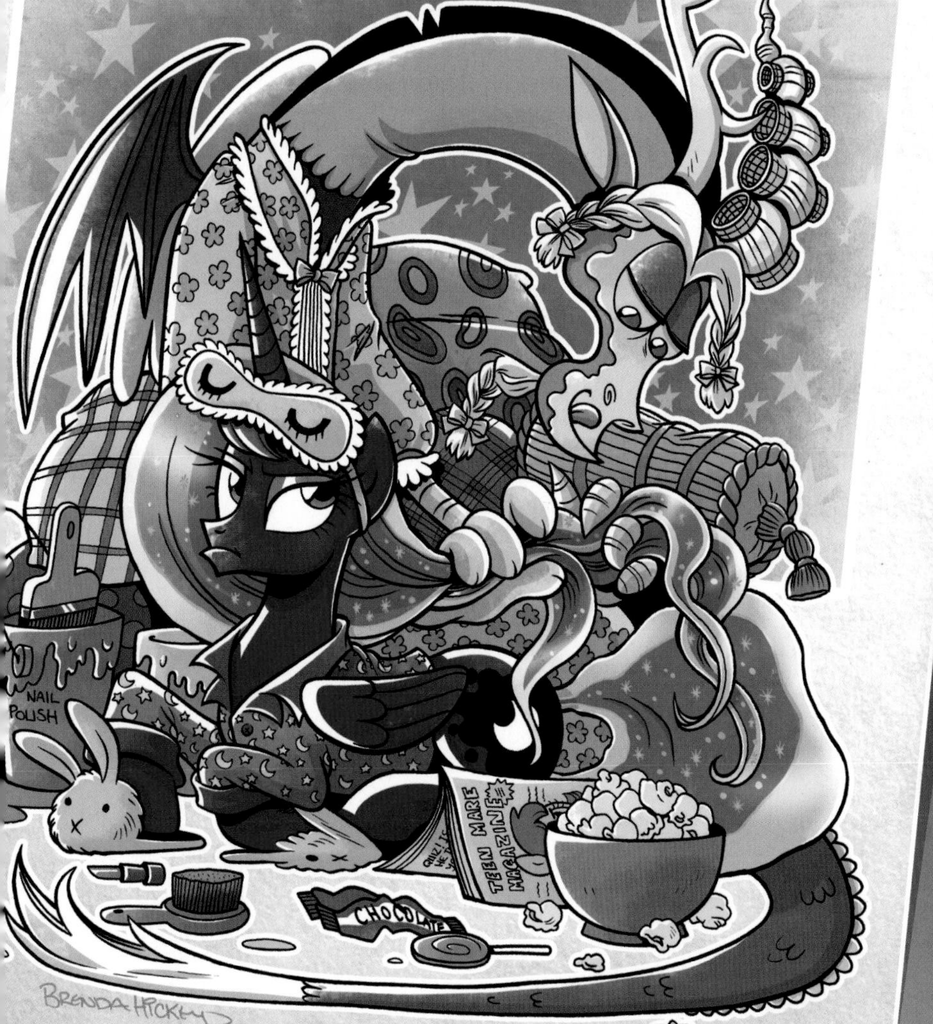
NAIL POLISH
TEEN MARE MAGAZINE
CHOCOLATE
BRENDA HICKEY

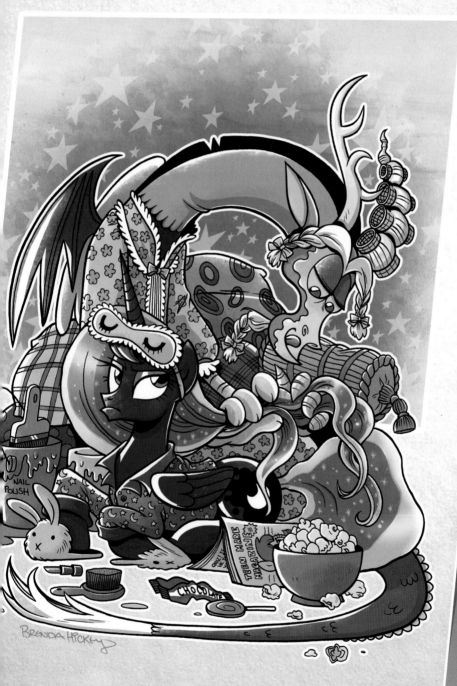

T BY **BRENDA HICKEY**

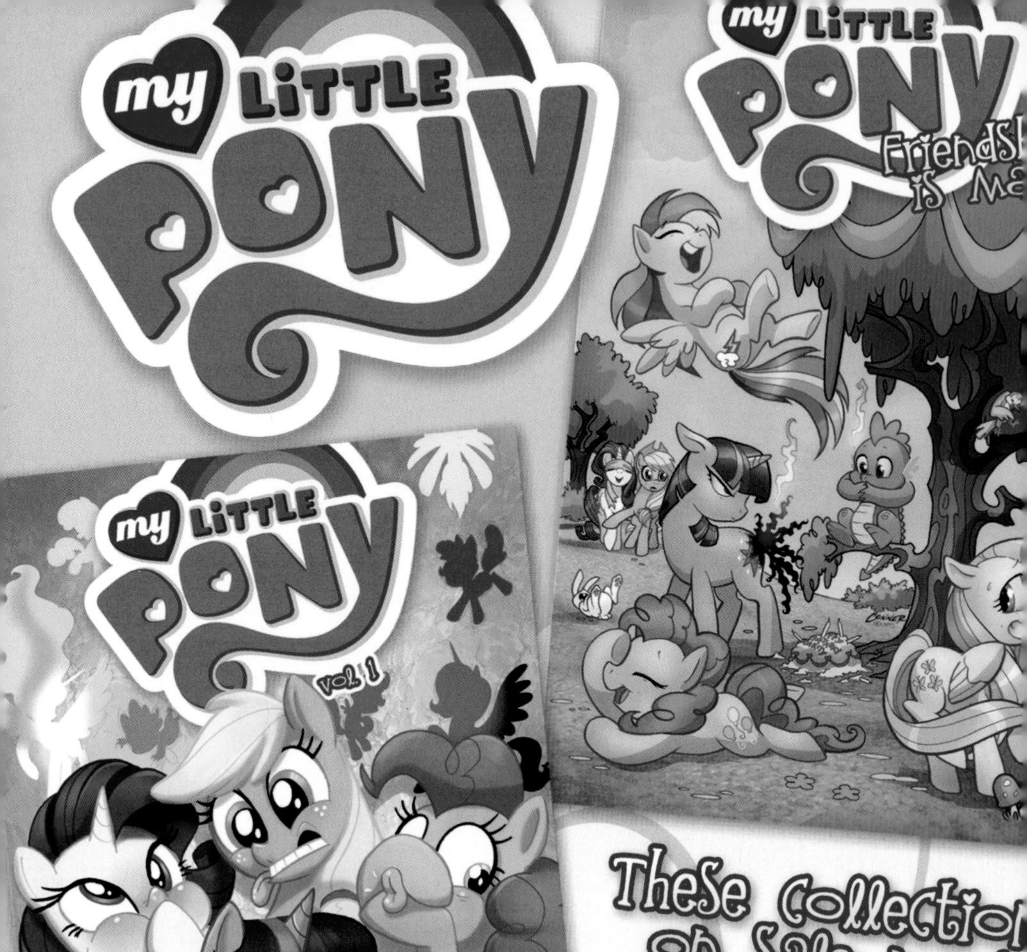
my LITTLE PONY
my LITTLE PONY Friends... is Ma...
my LITTLE PONY vol. 1
PONY TALES
These Collectio... on Sale now!

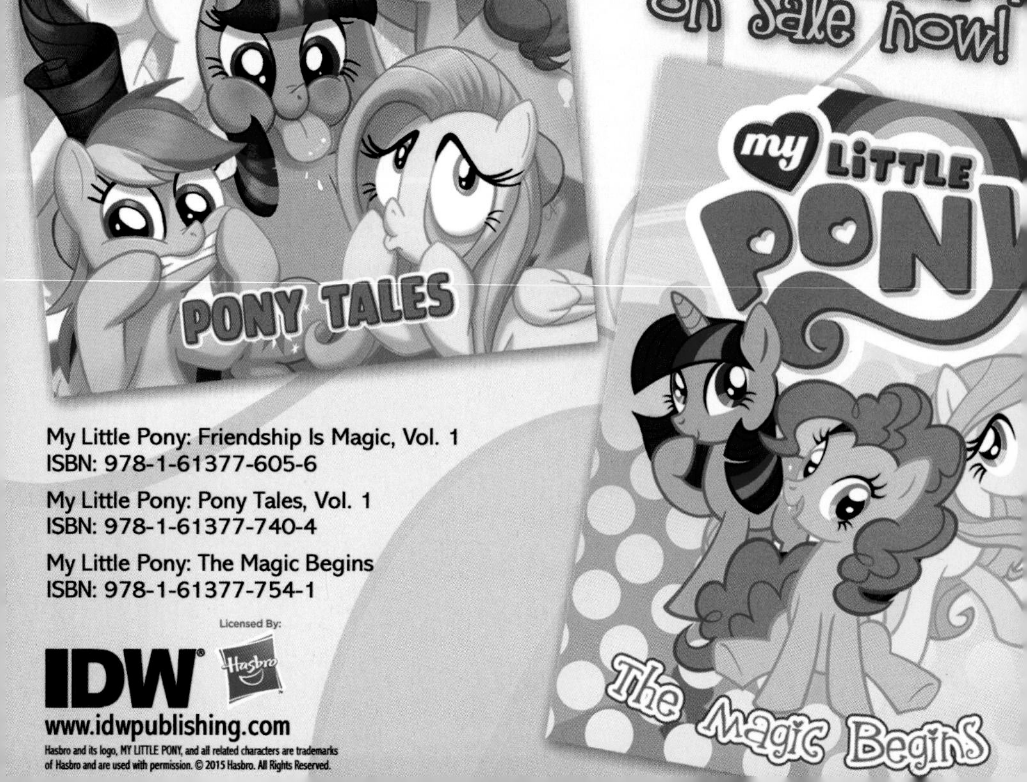
my LITTLE PON...
The Magic Begins

ISBN: 978-1-61377-605-6

ISBN: 978-1-61377-740-4

ISBN: 978-1-61377-754-1

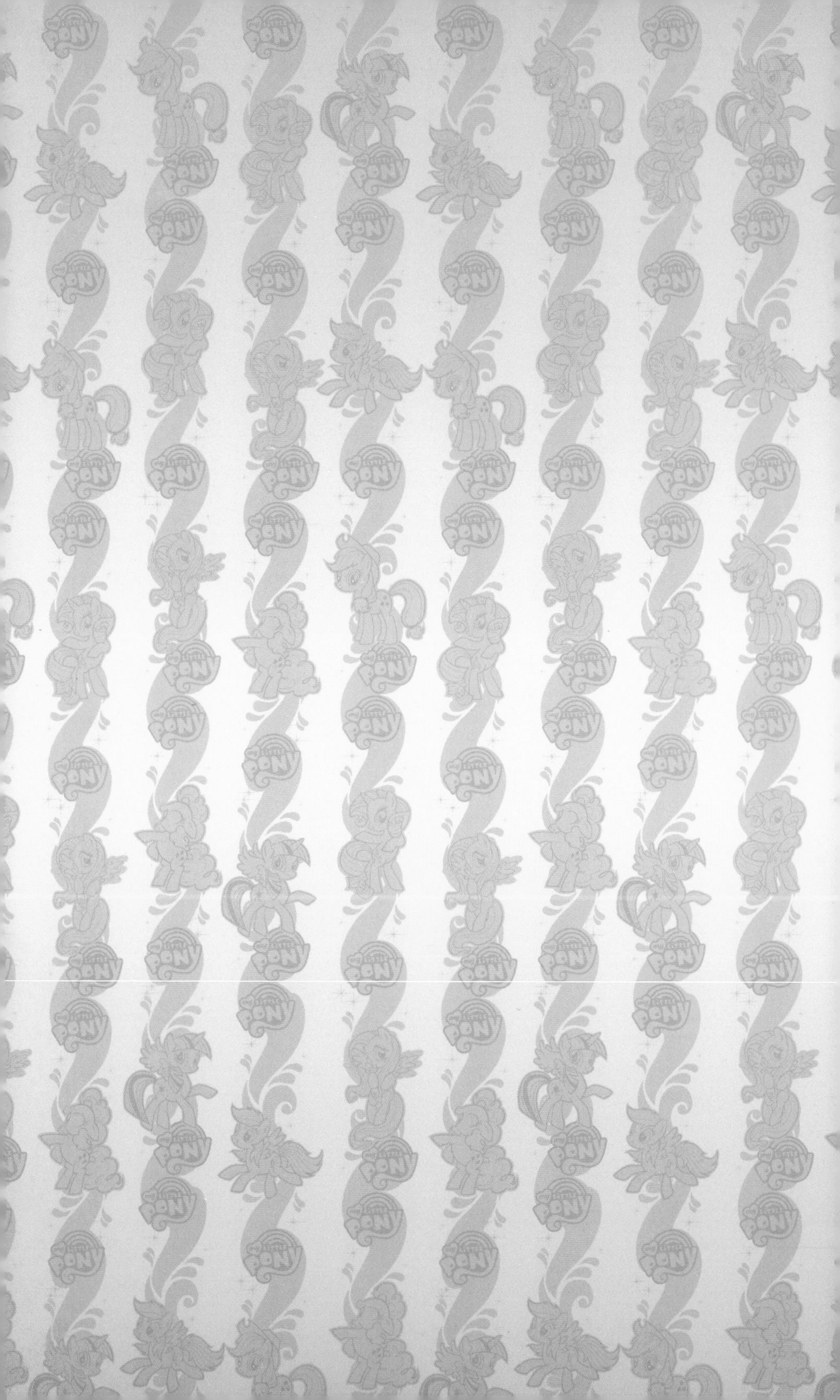